Michael swore about if he couldn't manage to belt the kilt in place, he'd walk out of the alley naked.

C.C. suppressed a giggle. "Are you sure you don't need my help?"

"If you promise not to laugh."

"I can't promise anything."

"Honesty. Fair enough."

She turned slowly, expecting…well, she wasn't sure what she expected. He had the wool fabric twisted loosely around his waist and draped over both shoulders. He held what looked like a death grip on the bunched fabric at his waist. "You seem to have the main idea," she said encouragingly. "And you're not naked."

"I will be if I let go. I can't get it to fit in place the right way."

She bit on her lip to keep from smiling. "How can I help?"

"If you can reach my belt…"

C.C. picked up the belt from the Campbell kilt on the ground. "You have the plaid too bunched up. You'll have to let go so I can readjust the fabric."

He lifted an eyebrow. "That wouldn't be a good idea."

"We'll go slowly, then." C.C. reached up to slip the wool down over his left shoulder. "If I can pull this through…" His breath was warm on her skin as she slipped it around and down.

"I'm the one who's done all this research, and yet you know how this type of kilt is worn. How is that possible?"

"Romance novels."

A Bride for a Day

by

Pam Binder

Matchmaker Café Series, Book Two

A Bride for a Day

Cover Art by *Kristian Norris*

The Wild Rose Press, Inc.
PO Box 708
Adams Basin, NY 14410-0708
Visit us at www.thewildrosepress.com

Publishing History
First Fantasy Rose Edition, 2017
Print ISBN 978-1-5092-1278-1
Digital ISBN 978-1-5092-1279-8

Matchmaker Café Series, Book Two
Published in the United States of America

Dedication

To my wonderful mother,
who created my fairytale wedding
with the man of my dreams.

Dreams become real
when they are shared with someone you love.

Chapter One

"You can't marry just anyone."

Michael Campbell caught the meaning of his friend's words as well as the snow-dusted football Harold had lobbed in his direction. *Settle down or risk everything you've fought to achieve.* It wasn't the first time someone had said that to him.

He waited as an elderly couple, dressed in wool coats and green plaid scarves, crossed in front of them on their way to the café and their morning cup of coffee. They probably wondered why two grown men were playing catch in the street on New Year's Eve. He shrugged. Sometimes old habits were all a person had left. With the couple inside, Michael arced the football back to Harold.

Funny that it had taken traveling to Scotland over the holidays to bring the topic of how to repair his reputation to a head. Like most professional football players, he lived large, or at least that was the story the press told. The truth didn't sell as many newspapers.

Harold returned the football, a wild throw arching dangerously close to the waters of the River Ness as it meandered along the perimeter of Inverness.

Michael jogged to make the catch. His friend's accuracy was not what it once had been. No matter. His friend had his back.

Harold Donavan had been his best friend since

grammar school. They'd played high school and college football together. They'd tossed the football back and forth while waiting for the bus and planning for the future. And as usual, Harold had a point. But not for the reasons his best friend thought.

Snow crunched under Harold's boots as he walked toward Michael. "I'm well aware of my situation," Michael said, heading back to position.

"I'm not sure you are." Harold stuffed his hands into the pockets of his wool overcoat. "Can we go inside? I'm freezing my briefs."

"Lawyer joke?"

"Fact. It's the dead of winter in Inverness, Scotland, and you're dressed like it's springtime in Florida."

Michael palmed the football in one hand and opened the door to the café for Harold with the other. "It's not that cold."

"Remind me. Why are we friends?"

"We never lie to each other."

Harold paused at the threshold of the café. Warm air and the earthy smell of brewed coffee and the hum of conversation beckoned. "And I'm not lying to you now. You have to marry the right person."

"Have you forgotten that I'm secretly engaged?"

"I've tried. Tatiana's divorce from her husband is still in the blame-game stage."

"I need coffee." Michael entered the café and headed toward a table overlooking the River Ness. There was a tent card on the table that read Reserved for Michael Campbell. He flipped the card onto its face. He couldn't escape his celebrity no matter how far he traveled. If he had known his life's trajectory, would he have made the same decisions?

He nodded his thanks to Fiona, the barista who brought their coffee. He'd heard Fiona was one of the new owners of the coffee shop who had recently changed its name from the Water Horse to the Matchmaker Café.

Harold joined him and slid into the chair opposite, also nodding his thanks to Fiona. He leaned forward. "Need I remind you that you are Michael Campbell, professional star quarterback, that you have a Super Bowl ring you never wear, and that you are up for the lead role in a major motion picture? A role, by the way, that you told me you wanted. Your football fans won't care who you marry, but the producers of this film do. You need an image adjustment. Marriage to the right person will solve that issue."

"You make it sound like I dislocated my shoulder and need to make sure I choose the right surgeon."

Harold blew on his coffee. "Now you get it. The world is changing. They like to see their heroes settled down and headed for happily-ever-after."

"There's no such thing."

Harold chuckled and looked over the rim of his cup. "Your grandmother would send you to your room without dinner for that remark."

"I'm sure she would." Michael took a drink of his coffee and glanced out the window. The waters of the River Ness shone like polished silver, as though lit from below by thousands of fires. Winter winds skimmed over the surface until the water sparkled like diamonds. On a day such as this, it was easy to imagine how legends, such as the Loch Ness Monster—Nessie, to her fans—had come into being.

And with each passing moment, more of the town woke in excitement to the realization that today was New Year's Eve. It was time to review the past year's resolutions and make way for the new. Michael didn't believe in fantasies or promises. Those were the dreams of children.

He took another swallow of his coffee. Was this the year he could stop running from his past?

Harold continued, breaking into Michael's thoughts. "Tatiana has made it clear that the two of you can't announce your engagement, let alone marry, until she's signed the divorce papers. So she's not an option."

Michael finished his coffee. "I know."

"If you ask me, Tatiana is deliberately inventing reasons to delay finalizing her divorce."

Michael remembered that his grandmother had made the same observation when she'd visited him last week for Christmas. "You keep telling me things I already know. You're the one who went to law school. Tell me something useful."

"We both were accepted into Stanford Law School. You're the one who chose a football career."

Michael tore his gaze from the river and scanned the crowded coffee shop. "Dreams change. You should know that better than anyone. You're doing your lawyer thing. You're changing the topic."

"So sue me. You look out for everyone, my friend. Someone has to look out for you." Harold reached into his briefcase and pulled out a folder. "My advice is that we choose an unknown for your bride. The press finds that romantic."

"The press feeds off scandals." Michael brought

his cup up to his lips, then remembered he'd finished his coffee.

"You're making my point. That's another reason for you to play it safe." Harold flipped open the folder. "She was right under our noses all along. Your girlfriend's assistant, C.C."

Michael clamped his jaws. "Out of the question." Michael started to rise from his chair. "I need a refill."

Harold reached out toward him. "Hold on. C.C. is perfect. A little plain, with out-of-control hair, no fashion sense, and mousey brown eyes, but we can glam her up. The 'ugly duckling transformed into a beautiful swan' fairy tale." Harold drained his coffee. "The press will eat it up. You usually go for the leggy model types. The big plus is that C.C. always smiles. That plays into our story that you need someone to lighten your stone-statue persona."

An image of C.C. burst into Michael's mind as though a door had opened. Outside of his grandmother, C.C. was the kindest person he knew. She had a way of adding sunshine to the gloomiest day. "Her eyes aren't mousey brown. They're more like warm honey, sometimes baked cinnamon."

Harold shoved his glasses up the ridge of his nose. "Okay. Good to know." He made a flourish of reaching for a pen in the inside pocket of his suit jacket and scribbling something in the margin. "I've made a note. Eyes change color." He gazed at Michael for a split second before turning the page. "Back to business. The best part is that we found out C.C. has a sick father."

Michael narrowed his gaze. Just yesterday C.C. had asked his help to coax a kitten out of tree. He'd almost broken his neck, but it had been worth it. But in all the time they'd spent together over the past three months, she'd never mentioned anything about her father, let alone that he was ill. "Why is C.C.'s father being sick a good thing?"

The brass bell over the front door chimed as Tatiana and her mother, Alba, made their grand entrance. They looked more like sisters than mother and daughter, and both were dressed in designer clothes in shades of gray and black. Tatiana's mother paused as though surveying her kingdom, motioned for Tatiana to find them a table, and then locked onto Michael.

Alba's high heels clattered on the wood floor as she headed his way. The woman was a bundle of sharp edges and judgment. Michael braced for the daily confrontation as she approached. He chided himself for his criticism. Alba had been a single mother raising a beautiful daughter. That couldn't have been easy. Especially when that daughter had attracted the attention of modeling agencies and powerful men. Alba was both manager and mother, orchestrating everything from modeling jobs to boyfriends, and always with the realization that in a blink it could all go away.

Alba reached Michael's table and pulled off her gloves. "Shouldn't you be getting ready for tonight's ceremony? Your wedding is this afternoon."

Michael turned to Harold and raised an eyebrow. "I'm getting married? Today?"

****

The sounds of the café closed in around him, ringing in his ears. He tried to calm the rising panic. He was getting married? Today? It was true that he was engaged to Tatiana and theoretically that meant that someday they would be husband and wife. If he were honest, he liked that she kept moving the date.

"You didn't tell him?" Alba said, in a shrill whisper.

"Alba. Could you give Michael and me a minute?"

Alba pulled her lips together into a thin line. "We don't have the luxury of time." She glanced over toward her daughter. Tatiana had a latte in each hand and was making her way to a vacant table near Michael's, avoiding his gaze.

Tatiana had been avoiding him since she'd returned from her visit with her soon-to-be-ex husband. Darrell Grant was a quarterback for a rival team and had a solid reputation on and off the field. Tatiana had never mentioned why she and Darrell had split, and it was none of Michael's business. "Aren't you and Tatiana joining us?" Michael said.

Ignoring Michael's question, Alba poked a finger into Harold's shoulder. "Convince your friend this is in all of our best interests and our only option. Do I have to remind you that we need to get this settled before my daughter changes her mind? Again." With a lift of her chin, she walked over to Tatiana's table.

When Alba was settled, Michael turned back to Harold. "Care to explain what that was all about?"

"I was getting around to it. As I mentioned, C.C. has a sick father."

Michael leveled his gaze at Harold. "Why is her father being sick good news? If you think that, then you're the one who's sick."

Harold adjusted his steel-gray tie. "Of course I'm not glad he's sick. However, this gives us an opportunity. Her father has leukemia and can't cover all of his medical expenses. C.C. is sending the majority of her paychecks to her brother and two sisters to help with his care. That means she's had to put off her dream. Care to guess what it is?"

"She's good with animals. They love her. She wants to be a veterinarian?"

"Isn't everyone good with animals?" Harold said.

"They hate you."

"Hilarious. No, smart guy, C.C. doesn't want to be a vet. She wants to open a sandwich shop. Like I said, our plan is perfect. We tell her that all she has to do is agree to enter into a fake marriage with you. We'll offer to give her a very generous bonus that will cover medical expenses for her father with enough left over to help her open the sandwich shop she's dreamed of. A small fortune for C.C. and her family, but the equivalent of a weekend shopping spree for Tatiana and her mother. The press will be convinced that you're ready to settle down and abandon your playboy ways. Your football contract will be renewed, and the movie deal to play the lead in *Highland Rebel* will be a sure thing. Then, after an acceptable amount of time has passed, we release a statement to the press that your marriage was a mistake. Something along the lines of the two of you being different people."

"That's an understatement."

"Good," Harold said. "We've reached common ground. By then, maybe Tatiana's divorce will be final, and you can marry your supermodel. The two of you can produce a litter of supermodels and football players. Everybody wins."

Michael watched his friend replace the folder in his briefcase. "Does Tatiana know?"

"It was her idea. Her mother doesn't like the plan.

Not sure why. However, Alba couldn't come up with anyone better suited at such short notice. We're up against a time constraint. The movie studio plans to make their decision the first of January."

The brass bell over the entrance to the Matchmaker Café chimed as the door opened again. C.C. entered, carrying a box that Michael knew was filled with sandwiches she had made. She'd shared one of her creations with the owners a few weeks ago, and they'd asked her to supply them with as many as she could make. He didn't know how she did it, but she managed to turn a simple sandwich into a must-have experience. Michael's favorite was the Swiss cheese and ham on rye.

Snow dusted her black wool coat and highlighted the cascade of dark wind-blown curls flowing over her shoulders. Michael started to get up to help her with her packages, but William, the older man from behind the counter, reached her first. William worked with Fiona and reminded Michael of a slim Santa Claus.

C.C.'s smile for William, as he took the box and carried it back to the counter, gave Michael a twinge of jealousy that William instead of himself was the recipient of such a smile. Why hadn't he been the one to help her?

Then she glanced toward Michael and smiled in acknowledgement of his presence. It felt as though his heart had stopped beating. Two thoughts flooded to the surface. The first was that her eyes this morning were the color of nutmeg, with a touch of gold highlights. The second was that he was in deep trouble.

Chapter Two

C.C. unwrapped her scarf from around her neck. The Matchmaker Café had become a morning tradition during their brief stay in Scotland. She stood near the entrance, drinking in the atmosphere. Warm air, laced with the earthy aroma of coffee, and the soothing hum of conversation greeted her like a close friend. The coffee shop seemed to whisper for her to take a breath and slow down. *Everything will be all right*, it seemed to say. *Your father is a strong man. He'll beat this.* She took in a ragged breath and straightened her shoulders. She needed coffee.

A few minutes ago she'd smiled over at Michael and received his signature stony stare. She didn't know why it bothered her so much that she couldn't get him to smile. She'd made it her mission and resorted to asking dumb football questions to see if she could break through his shell. Like why was a football called a pig-skin, or did the players really talk about football plays in the huddle or did they talk about who they were dating? Sometimes when she asked him a football question she thought she noticed a glimmer that might morph into a smile, but then it would disappear. She'd asked his grandmother last week, when she'd visited him on Christmas, why Michael was always so serious and if she knew of any way to make him smile. The wonderful woman had given C.C. a hug as the only response. C.C. was still trying to figure out what that had meant.

She shook her head. It wasn't her business. She had other issues to worry about. C.C. had noticed Tatiana and her mother huddled near Michael's table. She knew they wouldn't mind if she ordered her latte first before meeting with them for the morning briefing. Tatiana's mother insisted people around her be fully caffeinated at all times. C.C. sucked in a deep breath. She'd delayed long enough. Time to officially start her day. She unbuttoned her coat and headed over to the counter to place her order.

According to the archives at the library, the coffee shop and its rooms on the second and third floors had undergone numerous transformations over the past five hundred years. In the eighteenth century it had been a tavern, and a meeting place for the Jacobites, who supported Bonnie Prince Charlie. It was later turned into a hotel, a brothel, and then during World War II it became a hospital. From then until recently, it had been a pub called the Water Horse, named after the Loch Ness Monster, but the new owners—or lessees, actually—had renamed it the Matchmaker Café. The guidebooks joked that there were likely more pubs and coffee shops in Scotland than sheep.

C.C. reached the counter and was greeted by Fiona's smile and faint Scottish brogue. Fiona, along with her sisters Bridget and Lady Roselyn, had taken over the lease of the coffee shop. The young woman's blonde hair was pulled back into a ponytail, and she wore black rimmed glasses that instead of looking dorky reminded C.C. of her adorable younger sister, Rose.

A wave of homesickness struck C.C. so fast she had to reach out for the counter. How long had it been since she'd been home? Six months? A year? She gripped the counter tighter. It was closer to eighteen months.

"Are you all right?" Fiona said.

C.C. nodded. "I'm fine. I made an extra batch of sandwiches this morning. I thought with the holiday you might need them."

"You're a mind reader. We are expecting a crush of people today. Do you want your usual?"

C.C. nodded again, then glanced over at Michael as though pulled by an invisible thread. He and Harold were engrossed in conversation. She transferred her glance to Tatiana and her mother. They were equally absorbed. It was unusual that they weren't sitting together, but the habits of the rich and famous were a mystery that C.C. had long ago given up trying to decipher.

Today Tatiana looked even more carefully pulled together than normal, as though a photo shoot might be planned for later in the day. She had chiseled cheekbones, Cleopatra eyes, a skin-tight dress, and thigh-high boots. Her mother was just an older version and sat across from Tatiana checking her messages. C.C. suspected a soft center lay beneath Tatiana's sharp edges, if only she could get out from under her mother's watchful gaze. Again, none of C.C.'s business.

She turned back to Fiona, who had been waiting patiently. "Could I have extra whipped cream?" C.C. said.

"Of course. Chocolate sprinkles?"

"Absolutely."

When her latte was ready, she headed over to Tatiana's table, but Harold called her over to join him and Michael. She paused, waiting for Tatiana's slight nod of approval before making an about-face. At times like these she felt she walked a tight rope. Michael paid her salary, but he'd made it clear that C.C. worked for Tatiana and her mother.

Michael Campbell was six-foot-six and could intimidate anyone with a look. He was a professional quarterback who ate healthy, worked out like a crazy person, dated only models over six feet tall, and of course, the big one, never smiled.

Harold pulled a chair out for her. "C.C., we have a problem," he said, getting straight to the point. "The studio is waffling on offering our man the movie part for *Highland Rebel*. Even though we all traveled to Scotland to demonstrate Michael's commitment to this project, the studio isn't convinced. And Michael dating someone who is separated but not yet divorced hasn't helped eliminate his playboy image of dating only super-models with issues. We need a game change."

C.C. settled in the chair and glanced over at Tatiana and her mother. They had both stopped what they were doing and were concentrating on Harold. C.C. blew on her latte, trying to figure out why she'd been brought into this conversation. They'd hired her three months ago as Tatiana's assistant. Her duties had expanded to making Tatiana appear more likeable to the press. "The press likes to exaggerate. Besides, Michael has nailed the Scottish brogue, and he looks great in a kilt. That should count for something."

Harold slid a glance toward Michael and, after

receiving the go-ahead, said, "They mentioned words like 'heroic,' 'chivalrous,' and 'trustworthy.' They want the image of a one-woman man, like the character he would be playing. They don't want a man who trades in girlfriends as often as the weather changes in Scotland."

"A little harsh, my friend," Michael said.

Harold shrugged.

C.C.'s latte was still too hot to drink, and she blew on it again, playing for time. She looked over at Tatiana. The woman was leaning forward as though awaiting C.C.'s response. C.C. glanced toward Michael. He was busy shredding his napkin.

She concentrated on her latte. The whipped cream was dissolving into the coffee, turning it the color of milk chocolate. "Why don't we leak it to the press that Michael and Tatiana will be announcing they are getting married? They're already planning on attending the New Year's Eve party tonight at the MacBride Mansion. We can turn it into an engagement party. Michael has a kilt, and he can impress them with his accent. Tatiana will look gorgeous. They'll have the press eating out of their hands."

Harold exchanged a glance with Michael. "We can't. Tatiana's divorce isn't final. She said her husband would only make things more difficult if he knew her relationship with Michael was serious."

She glanced over at Michael again. He had clenched his jaw and was focused on his empty coffee cup. C.C. had seen that look before—on the football field when he'd disagreed with a play the coach had called.

Harold smiled, but the smile looked pasted on with tape. "We have something else in mind."

Michael braided his fingers around his cup. "This isn't going to work out the way you think, Harold."

"It will," Harold insisted. "All we have to do is stay focused on the end game."

C.C. looked from Michael to Harold. Harold wasn't just Michael's manager; they'd been best friends since Michael had rescued Harold from the neighborhood bullies in grammar school. This was the first time she'd seen them disagree. If they had differences, they always kept them private and showed a united front in public.

"What's going on?" C.C. said.

Michael looked toward her and held her gaze. "Harold wants the two of us to get married. Tonight."

Chapter Three

All the oxygen must have been sucked out of the coffee shop, C.C. thought. The lights seemed brighter and the voices louder. She kept her eyes down, avoiding eye contact. Was it her imagination or had everyone in the café overheard what Michael had said? The customers in the coffee shop seemed to be holding their breath—or was she the one who had trouble breathing?

Her hand shook as she brought her cup to her lips and then set it back down untouched. Michael and Harold were discussing the wedding details as though she'd already agreed. There was the mention of a generous bonus. Half now, and half when they divorced. She wasn't opposed to the idea of marriage. She expected one day she'd get around to it when she met the right man.

She heard snippets of conversation from Michael and Harold as though the sound came from a long way away. They talked about how best to make the announcement to the press, including a story about how Michael and C.C. had managed to keep their romance a secret. Their first choice was to have the wedding take place at the mansion. All they needed was permission from the owners, which Harold didn't see as a problem. After all, the owners of the mansion also ran the Matchmaker Café.

C.C.'s logical side applauded the plan. They had all the details worked out. It was hard to tell what Michael was thinking, which was pretty standard. He nodded a lot. Harold was busy making lists and said he would make the arrangements for authentic Scottish food and music. All that was left was hiring someone to play the part of a minister and purchasing a wedding dress for C.C. He asked C.C. if she had a preference about whether she was "fake" married by a justice of the peace, a minister, a rabbi, or a priest. She shook her head slowly and concentrated on her latte.

Her mind reeled. They wanted her to marry Michael. Why hadn't they asked Tatiana? It didn't make sense. She needed space to think this through. She took a few deep breaths and started to stand, but Harold reached for her arm, and she eased back into her chair. His nod seemed to say that everything would be okay. She understood this would be a fake wedding. After a few months, six at the most, they'd tell the world that things hadn't worked out. So why was the whole idea freaking her out?

"C.C.," Harold said, "did you hear my question? What size dress do you wear? And do you want white or a cream shade?" He eyed her coat. "I hear some brides prefer wearing colors these days."

"I don't know." Hands trembling, she brought her latte to her lips, but she was shaking so much she had to use both hands to steady the cup. The hot liquid sloshed over the rim, spilling over her sleeve, and its heat seeped through the thin fabric. White-hot pain seared over her skin. Feeling numb, she stared as her drink spread over the sleeve covering her arm and blended into the black cloth.

Michael jumped to his feet and pulled the chair with C.C. still seated on it out from under the table. "We need water," he shouted. "And ice."

She looked at her arm as though it belonged to someone else. "I'm fine," she insisted. "It doesn't hurt that much."

"You're not fine." Not waiting for help, he lifted her from the chair and hurried past gaping customers and behind the counter toward the sink, where he turned on the cold water.

Fiona was at his side immediately with a bag of ice, asking if he thought she should call a doctor.

He shook his head. "I think we'll be okay. I'll know in a minute." He set the ice pack aside and slowly pulled C.C.'s sleeve away from the burn. He took a deep breath as he positioned C.C. so she faced the sink and put his arms around her to guide her arm under the water. "Good, the cloth didn't stick," he said, meeting C.C.'s gaze. "This might sting a little." Without waiting for an answer, he shoved her arm under the running water.

She felt warm in his arms, but her teeth still clattered together. "I'm such a klutz."

A muscle twitched along his temple as his gaze focused on her burn. "You don't have to marry me. We'll think of something else."

She knew there were others in the café, but it felt as though it were just the two of them. They were so close. His chest was pressed against her side. She swallowed. Concentrate. This was a business deal. Harold thought the plan would help Michael, and the money they offered would really help her father. Her arm felt numb under the cold water, giving her time to process. This was a business deal, she rationalized again. Win-win for everyone concerned. What could possibly go wrong?

She glanced over at Tatiana. The woman in question was staring in C.C.'s direction. But it was her mother's expression that chilled C.C. to the bone. It looked like it could cut glass. C.C. shuddered. "Why don't you marry Tatiana?"

Michael sucked in a deep breath. "It's complicated."

"Do you really believe our marriage will improve your image?"

"Harold seems to think so."

"But I'm not your type." She felt his chest rumble in something suspiciously like a chuckle. Did he find what she'd said humorous? Or ironic?

"Because the press will believe you're not my type," Michael said, "is precisely why Harold thinks it will work."

She knew he believed his potential movie deal had fallen into his lap, and that he was curious where it might lead. He hadn't sought it out, but in classic Michael Campbell fashion, he'd not backed away from the challenge. However, she knew he wasn't going to give up football just yet. He'd told her that he'd seen other athletes quit their sport too soon, chasing a dream, from starting a restaurant to a new line of clothes. In some cases, their new ventures had crashed and burned. Sometimes the fans had followed them. Most of the time the athlete was forgotten the moment he or she stepped off the field. She had to give Michael credit. He had refused to give up his sport until he knew for sure he could make it as an actor.

She knew asking him anything personal was a waste of time. She stayed on safe ground while she slipped her arm from his grasp.

Michael turned off the water and reached for a towel. "How does your arm feel?"

"Better. You know, actually, Harold's marriage idea has merit, and choosing me as your fiancée fits perfectly. I'm the type that can fade into the background and let you shine. A marriage will signal to the movie producers that you've settled down and are more serious. The studio will love that you chose the Scottish Highlands as the setting for your wedding and will be figuring out how to tie it into the movie when it's released next year." She paused. "Where did you learn how to treat a burn?"

"My grandmother. I was helping her make breakfast and reached for the handle of a fry pan without using a hot pad." He rubbed the palm of his hand. "I still have a small scar."

She resisted the impulse to touch his hand. "I always thought that would have been tough, losing both your parents when you were so young. I have a large family, and we don't always get along, but we are always there for each other."

"You don't miss what you never had." He reached for the ice pack. "Look. I agree that Harold's plan sounds solid, but who's going to believe the two of us are a couple? I mean..."

"I'm not your type," she finished, not taking offense. After all, she'd brought up the point herself. She felt like he and Tatiana dwelled in an alternate universe. They were the prince and princess of the fairytale, while she was a peasant in the village. Only in this case there wasn't going to be a fairy godmother and a magic pumpkin coach. That only happened in books and in the movies. She glanced over toward Tatiana and her mother again. They looked so perfect. They were bent together in conversation, but whatever they were discussing, it was clear they weren't in agreement. But even in disagreement they looked perfect. Almost like poetry. When she and her siblings fought, it was not pretty.

C.C. glanced away and continued. "I'm the girl-next-door. Your type is the international model who is out of most men's league. The studio and the press will see our marriage as a sign that you really are settling down. Harold's plan is flawless."

Michael stuffed his hands in his jean pockets. "That's what has me worried."

Chapter Four

The MacBride mansion stood watch over Inverness and the restless waters of the River Ness. Inside the Victorian-style home, Lady Roselyn, the eldest of the three matchmaker sisters, sipped her tea. She glanced out the bay window, enjoying the view. Clouds hung low over the city, covering building cranes and modern steel-and-concrete office skyscrapers. From her vantage point, it was easy to imagine the city as it had been hundreds of years ago.

The morning was overcast and gray, but it was, after all, the dead of winter in the Scottish Highlands. Tea steamed in her cup and a double fudge brownie rested on a china plate handpainted with blue and yellow wildflowers. The perfect combination for days like these. She didn't mind the weather. The Highlands had been her family's home for centuries.

It had felt natural to take over the lease of the coffee shop and set up residence in the mansion her ancestors had built so long ago. After the near disaster at Stirling Castle on Christmas Eve, their move here had taken the better part of a week, and the majority of their things were still in crates. Sadly, she knew the move to their ancestral home was only a temporary stopover. They were scheduled to open a Matchmaker Café in the United States shortly after the start of the New Year. One of their cousins would operate the one here in Inverness. Even so, she was glad they were here, if only for a short time. In this relaxed atmosphere she hoped her sisters, Fiona and Bridget, would share what was really troubling them.

She took a sip of tea and then reached for her fork. She deserved a little "me time," as the Americans would say.

"Are you crazy?"

Her brownie untouched, she heaved a sigh and put the fork down, turning toward Bridget. Her sister stood framed in the doorway of the parlor. A flyer was clutched in her hand. She was dressed casually in pressed jeans, an oversized white sweater, and leg-hugging boots. Her hair was piled loosely on top of her head, and her blue eyes looked like they were about to ignite.

Lady Roselyn took another fortifying sip of tea. "Yes, I'm probably crazy; we all are, a little. Why else would we be matchmakers? But to what exactly are you referring?"

Marching over to Lady Roselyn, Bridget threw the flyer onto the table in front of her. "Do you remember our conversation in which I said we should skip the New Year's Eve party this year? We'll never be ready in time. We're still unpacking. And that's another thing. On Christmas Eve you said we were going to take a vacation. Somewhere warm. The old family home in Scotland, in the dead of winter, hardly qualifies."

Lady Roselyn drummed her fingers on the table as Bridget sat down opposite her. She could almost hear their mother's voice cautioning her to be patient with her younger sister. It was obvious that something else was bothering her. Pulling together matchmaking events on short notice was their specialty. Plus, Bridget loved the Highlands as much as they all did. One thing was certain. Bridget was itching for a fight. But why?

Carefully, Lady Roselyn picked up the flyer her sister had thrown on top of her chocolate brownie and scraped the frosting off with her napkin. Such a waste. "Yes, I remember all your objections when I announced the party. Did you hear any of the reasons why we had no choice in the matter? Starting with the most important one: Our family has held a New Year's Eve celebration for hundreds of years, and I will not be the first generation to break the tradition." She licked frosting off her fingers, envying those of her friends who were only children. "But I can understand why you didn't hear what was being said. You and Fiona were too busy arguing. There will be a New Year's Eve celebration tonight. This is the one event where we're not concerned with matching couples. The whole purpose is for people to have fun. Out with the old and in with the new. A chance to make a fresh start." She paused. "Our guests will be arriving soon, so I suggest you get dressed."

Bridget leaned across the table and placed both hands on the lace cloth. "No matchmaking, you say? Someone should have let Fiona know. William called and said our dear sister agreed to hold a wedding here this afternoon."

"That's a lovely idea. But a wedding hardly qualifies as a matchmaking event. The couple in question are getting married. They've already committed to each other. You're on edge for no reason. Please sit down and have some of my brownie."

Bridget obliged her sister and broke off a corner of

the brownie and took a bite. The chocolate seemed to calm her. "You're right. I'm sorry. I'm not sure why I overreacted."

Lady Roselyn reached over to take Bridget's hand, hoping she was wrong about the real reason Bridget was a bundle of nerves these days. "Nonsense. You wear your emotions on your sleeve, which is why we all love you. Moving so quickly was frustrating for us all, and so it's only natural that we are a little on edge. But I felt it best for us to leave Stirling Castle and its access to the thirteenth century. There's something going on with Fiona, and I'm worried that the castle's Brigadoon-like enchantment had something to do with it."

Bridget took another bite. "She doesn't want to marry Liam."

There was something in the tone of Bridget's voice when she mentioned Liam's name. The man quickened the blood, that was for sure. It was the rare woman who could remain immune to his easy smile and broad shoulders. But Lady Roselyn didn't believe Bridget was infatuated with the lad. The concern was that Fiona and Liam were constantly fighting, which was the reason their wedding had been delayed so many times. Bridget and Liam, however, got along wonderfully well. They agreed on everything, with never a cross word. If only Liam's parents had betrothed him to Bridget instead of Fiona. But what was done was done. Tradition decreed that when there were three daughters, the oldest and youngest would be married, while the middle child remained single. Bridget was the middle child.

Over the years there'd been pockets of rebellion, but their family had always upheld the old ways, and she wasn't about to be the first to break the chain. She added a heaping spoonful of sugar to her tea. "Is that what you argued with Fiona about? Her marriage to Liam?"

Bridget wiped her mouth on a linen napkin. "Not this time. Fiona was concerned we hadn't installed the right doors." Bridget took another bite. "This brownie is delicious. Did you make it?"

Lady Roselyn nodded slowly as she gazed out the window at the mist-shrouded day. The sun was doing its best to break through the thin cloud layer. Time would tell which was going to win. Time. She leaned closer to the window, feeling the cold air seep through the glass panes.

She and her sisters had a unique matchmaking system. Long ago, when the system had first been developed, their family believed that it wasn't enough to place two attractive people together and hope for the best. The real test of a lasting relationship was how a couple worked together when they were faced with conflict. Lady Roselyn was still not sure how the enchantment worked. Or how their clan had been gifted with it in the first place. That secret was entrusted to William, and his ancestors, and he was sworn to secrecy.

The doors were of various sizes and shapes, and had once been in castles, manor houses, and places all over the globe. Once installed, they could open to the place and date etched or painted on the door. The enchanted doors she and her sisters had inherited played a major role. It was intriguing that Fiona had been so concerned about which ones were installed.

She turned back to Bridget. "Did Fiona mention

which door she was looking for?"

Bridget reached across the table to take a sip of Lady Roselyn's tea. "No, but she was pretty frantic. She was concerned that we might have left some of them behind. I told her that wouldn't happen. I made the joke that William was our Keeper of the Doors and had them all catalogued. Leaving one behind for him would be like forgetting to pack one of his hats."

"What did she say?"

Bridget stood. "She didn't answer. She just stormed off. I should get dressed and check on the menu for tonight. If we're going to have a wedding, we'll need a cake. Again, I'm sorry for my outburst. I think you're right. This matchmaking business makes us all a little crazy from time to time."

Lady Roselyn straightened the napkin on her lap. "Don't worry about it."

Bridget nodded, turned to leave, but paused. "Oh, and thank you for the brownie."

Lady Roselyn glanced at the china plate. Only crumbs remained. Yes, there were days when she definitely envied her friends who were only children.

Chapter Five

Michael was admitted to the mansion's library with the message that Tatiana had asked to speak with him. She must have been reading his mind. He'd felt they were growing apart for the past several months. Since she'd returned from her visit with her soon-to-be ex-husband, Darrell Grant, she'd been different. Or maybe Michael was the one who was different. He fully expected Tatiana to break off their engagement, with the classic line, "It's not you, it's me."

As he entered, Tatiana was in the library facing a dark fireplace. "You wanted to see me?"

"I've changed my mind."

He waited for her to turn around and face him. Her statement could mean anything from the latest marketing plan for her shoe company to a shopping spree with her mother. Ever since Tatiana had visited her husband over Thanksgiving she'd been distant. Michael had understood. Divorcing someone you'd been married to for five years couldn't be easy.

She turned around, and in the shadows it looked as though she'd been crying. "I know I said I wanted to plan a big wedding." She dabbed at her eyes with a handkerchief. "But we'll get married as soon as my divorce is final."

Michael stuffed his hands in his pockets. He'd never seen Tatiana like this before. She rarely showed emotion, let alone tears. "What's wrong?"

She clutched the handkerchief in her hand. "My mother said Darrell is dating someone. Someone he wants to marry. My mother didn't know her name, but I think it's that model from New Zealand; Kiki is her name. Kiki actually told me once how jealous she was of me because I was married to a man like Darrell."

Michael wanted to point out that she and Darrell had been separated for almost two years and she herself was dating, after all. Tatiana had begun pacing across the room, almost wearing a pattern in the thick pile carpeting. Instinct told him that now wouldn't be the time to point out those little details.

She came to an abrupt stop and burst out, "I'm pregnant."

Michael felt a blast of heat hit him as though he'd walked into a furnace room. His first impulse was to grab her and tell her how happy he was. She didn't look happy, though. She looked prickly. Annoyed.

He moved toward her cautiously, as though she were a frightened animal that might run if he moved too fast. "All the more reason we should get married right away."

She wrung her hands together. "Don't you see? Darrell will never give me a divorce now. We said things. We did..." She flopped down on the sofa. "You and C.C. getting married is the only way. He's being stubborn. I told him I wanted the seaside cottage we lived in when we were first married. I can't stand the idea of Kiki sleeping in our bed. That's where we planned...where we hoped..."

Michael sat down beside her, and reached for her hand. "Do you still want a divorce?"

She sprang from the sofa. "What an odd thing to say! Didn't you hear what I was saying? Of course I want a divorce from Darrell. I know him. He won't meet my demands as long as you and I are dating. He said as much at Thanksgiving. He's crazy jealous of you. His contract wasn't renewed, and he has few options after two shoulder surgeries. Your career is on the rise." Her voice rose to a high pitch. "Don't you see? He won't give me what I want as long as we're together. That's why it has to look as though you've moved on and are married to someone else." She frowned. "He'll love the idea that you broke my heart."

This wasn't the first time Tatiana had accused Darrell of seeing other women. Her mother kept Tatiana well informed. It wasn't Michael's business, but it never made sense. True, Darrell was a competitor on the football field, but Michael liked the guy. If anything, it was rumored that Darrell still loved Tatiana and hadn't seen anyone since their breakup. That was the real reason Darrell was jealous of him and was being so stubborn.

"It's just a cottage," Michael said. "We can buy another one."

He knew the moment he'd said the words that they were the wrong ones to say. Her shoulders slumped forward as she buried her face in her hands. He'd heard that pregnant women sometimes were more emotional than normal. If this was what she wanted, then this was what he would help her get.

Michael rose and put his arm around her shoulders and pulled her against him. There was more going on than a cottage. He knew that without asking. Tatiana had never known the identity of her father. In Michael's case, his deadbeat dad had fled the moment he'd learned Michael's mother was pregnant. "Do you really think this fake marriage will work?"

She tilted her face to his. It was tearstained, and smudged with makeup. "Thank you. I'll have to make a scene at the wedding. Pretend like I'm hurt."

"I know."

He gathered her closer. It hit him that he'd entered into the realm of pretense. Everyone was pretending. Tatiana would pretend that she was outraged that Michael was getting married. He and C.C. would pretend to get married. When the dust settled, he and Tatiana would pretend they loved each other for the sake of their child. The only thing he wasn't pretending was how he felt about C.C.

Chapter Six

The grandfather clock, in the room Lady Roselyn referred to as the Door Room, struck five. She stood gazing out the window at the front entrance to the mansion. Guests were already gathering. At least something was going right. The habit of gazing out windows, she decided, was becoming too common of late. The consequences of their profession, she supposed. Below, a young woman was getting out of a limo with Fiona.

"That's the bride?"

William nodded.

"She's lovely."

"Fiona and C.C. spent the day shopping for dresses but couldn't find any that would suit."

"Understandable. Fiona told me that this is a marriage of convenience, so the bride-to-be is a little uncertain. I suggest we loan C.C. one in our collection. The Victorian lace, perhaps. What do you know of the groom?"

"Fine lad, but almost as nervous as the bride."

"Really? Well, now isn't that interesting?"

William scrunched his eyebrows together. "Why are you smiling?"

"You'll see. You'll see."

****

Several hours later, Inverness, Scotland, was

dressed up for New Year's Eve. Twinkling lights outlined shops, hotels and boats docked along the River Ness. The lights traveled around tree trunks, shimmered from their branches, and then outlined the bridges that joined the old section of Inverness with the new. A fairyland of infinite possibilities: out with the old and in with the new.

Inside the MacBride mansion overlooking the town, C.C. held in her lap the shoes Fiona had given her. Since the morning's unexpected decision at the Matchmaker Café, she'd felt as though she'd been caught in a strange whirlwind of dress shopping and wedding preparations. When the wedding shops in Inverness had not produced anything she'd liked, Fiona had driven them both to the mansion with the promise of a surprise, compliments of the matchmaker sisters.

C.C. knew it would be a dress. She didn't know it would be one that fulfilled every childhood dream she'd ever had. The gown hanging on the mannequin before her looked as though it had been made for a princess: white lace over satin, seed pearls, diamond-like crystals... She sucked in her breath. She'd wanted to refuse, think of an excuse like she had with the other dresses, but this one was so lovely. Her romantic side betrayed her by urging her to sigh and twirl around in a circle like a lovestruck sixteen-year-old before taking her seat.

Fiona opened a white box and selected a lace garter with a heart-shaped silver locket. "You haven't said a word in over half an hour."

"This is really happening."

Fiona scrunched her eyebrows together. "You look a little overwhelmed. Did I go overboard? I do that sometimes. I love weddings and wanted you to feel like Cinderella."

C.C. winced at the reference. Few knew that C.C. stood for Cinderella Charming. She looked down at the shoes she held. They looked like how she imagined Cinderella's glass slippers might look, which to most would feel like a fantasy come to life. To her, it was the direct opposite. The cloth on the shoes was almost transparent, and studded with crystals. Silver dusted the heels, and on each shoe perched a three-dimensional butterfly outlined in silver and gold threads.

"It's too much," C.C. said.

Fiona knelt down beside her and took both C.C.'s hands in hers. "We are aware that this wedding is all for show, but your bridegroom said that you don't have to go through with it. He's quite a guy, by the way."

C.C. lifted her gaze. "Have you noticed that everyone is in awe of celebrities, from movie and TV stars to athletes and multi-billionaires? Before modern time, it was the nobles. It's as though someone sprinkled them with magic fairy dust and turned them into super beings—we can't look away. We have to follow them, dream of meeting them. For the first time in my life I think I know what Cinderella must have been feeling. The fantasy is that she was excited and anxious to meet the prince, but I've always wondered if she was caught up in the romance of meeting a handsome guy everyone considered perfect and never really believed it would happen. There's safety in wanting something you know in your heart you can't have. When she realized it might really happen, she must have been in a panic. By then it was too late to turn back. Her path had been chosen for her. The prince was in a tenuous position as well. He had to choose a bride or risk losing the crown. Cinderella must have seemed like a breath of fresh air compared to the clingy royal princesses that only wanted him for his wealth and position. This evening Michael and I will exchange our vows, and tomorrow, or very soon afterwards, the marriage will be annulled. I'm a bride for a day. I don't know why this is bothering me so much. We don't love each other. We've struck a bargain. Our marriage helps his image, and I receive a generous bonus that will help my family. Everybody wins."

Fiona squeezed C.C.'s hands and came around to sit beside her. "You might find this strange, but I know exactly how you feel. Michael said much the same thing, and yet…"

C.C. looked up. "And yet…what?"

"Oh, nothing. Well, then, since the two of you want to make a good impression, we'd better get you ready."

"Do you have any wedding dresses in black?"

Chapter Seven

C.C. stood in the middle of the dressing room, afraid to sit down and crush the train of her gown. Fiona had left to see if everything was ready. This was the first time she'd been alone all day. A soft knock at the door drew her attention.

"Come in," she said, wondering why Fiona would knock.

The door opened to Alba, Tatiana's mother. At a quick glance, there was a close resemblance between Alba and her daughter. That stopped the moment either of them spoke or moved. Tatiana seemed to flow into a room, like a meadow stream. Alba burst in like a storm-fed river.

Alba took in C.C.'s appearance from the tip of her bare toes to the diamond-like accents tucked into C.C.'s long hair. "My daughter said she loaned you a pair of shoes. Why haven't you put them on? Or are you planning to walk down the aisle barefoot like a gypsy?"

"Gypsies wear shoes. I...I just haven't put them on yet."

Alba flipped open the shoebox on the table. "Interesting choice. I would have chosen something simpler from her collection. No matter. Be sure when the reporters ask you what you're wearing that you tell them these were made by Tatiana."

C.C. wanted to scream, *Why are you here*? Instead

she opted for diplomacy and reached for the shoes. "I won't forget."

Alba tucked in her chin. "It should be my daughter marrying Michael, not you."

"I agree."

"Don't get any ideas once you and Michael exchange vows."

"It's all make-believe. We won't really be getting married."

Alba opened her purse and took out a red lipstick, then turned toward the floor-length mirror and applied it to her mouth. "You will be spending a lot of time with Michael. The both of you will be pretending that you are in love." She smacked her lips together. "People can sometimes get confused as to what is real and what is a part they are playing. I think that's why so many actors get involved with their co-stars. Even my daughter suffers from that delusion. I think that's the reason she's having difficulty divorcing her husband so she can marry Michael. But her husband represents the past. Darrell's star power has burned out. Michael's will eclipse the sun."

"I know the difference between what is real and what is pretend. You don't have to worry."

"Worry? About you?" Alba peered closer to the mirror and brushed a smudge of makeup from under her eye. "Don't be absurd. It's Michael who has to be reminded about his commitments and that we know a secret he wants to stay hidden. He asked my daughter to marry him, and we intend him to follow through on his promise. If he thinks he has an image problem now, he'll think it was nothing more than an annoying splinter in his big toe compared to the onslaught of injuries we'll create if he goes back on his word." Alba fluffed her hair and turned to face C.C. "Are we clear?"

C.C. nodded. She'd read Michael's biography before she interviewed for the job, even though technically Tatiana would be her employer. There was nothing in his history that suggested dark secrets. In fact, he was a perfect example of how if you worked hard miracles happened. But everyone had secrets they wanted to keep hidden. Some were small, like binge-eating chocolate ice cream topped with chocolate sauce and chocolate sprinkles when your boyfriend dumped you for a skinnier version. What dark secret was Michael hiding?

Fiona walked into the room and gazed back and forth between C.C. and Alba. "Is everything all right in here?"

"We're just going over a few ground rules," Alba informed her.

Chapter Eight

Michael waited in a small room a short distance from the ballroom where the wedding was to take place. Once C.C. had agreed, Harold had moved at warp speed to make sure everything was done. Michael wondered how C.C. was doing. He kept waiting for that rush of panic to set in, or that feeling of being trapped. None of that had happened.

"Is that the wedding ring?" Tatiana slipped into the room and headed over to the sofa where he sat.

He tore his gaze from the gold band he held, a princess-cut diamond in its center. "Hello, Tatiana."

"Hello, yourself. You look good in the kilt. Are those your family's colors?"

He nodded and tucked the ring into his jacket pocket.

She sat down next to him, perching on the sofa like a bird on a wire. "The diamond is small and not to my taste, but it suits C.C. Did you buy it in town?"

He moved over to make space for her and shook his head. "It was my grandmother's. She gave it to me when she visited at Christmas. I told her I'd already bought you a ring, but she told me to keep it anyway. Are you ready?"

She crossed her legs and adjusted her short skirt. "Harold gave me a script to memorize, and he leaked to the press that you have a big announcement tonight."

She pulled a gold chain from her neck from which hung a ring with a large marquee-cut diamond surrounded by rubies and emeralds. She kissed him on the cheek and then wiped her red lipstick off his skin. "In a few short months, all of this will be behind us, and we can get married. I'll have my divorce, and you will have the love and respect of the whole world." She straightened her skirt again. "My mother likes the idea of our getting married at a castle in Scotland. The press will eat it up. We should ask the sisters to help with the preparations. They've done a great job here on such short notice. I'm not sure I like the food choices, but then, I'm not the one getting married."

Tatiana continued talking about the flowers and that she'd caught a glimpse of C.C.'s gown and that it was a little old-fashioned, and how some people liked that sort of thing. He leaned back, watching her fidget with her skirt and then tuck the chain with the engagement ring he'd given her back into her cleavage. She was beautiful. That was without question. He'd asked her to marry him, and she'd said yes. That had been over eight months ago. Had they ever loved each other?

Harold ducked his head into the room. "Michael. It's time."

Chapter Nine

C.C. stood outside the double doors to the ballroom, listening to the soft music as she waited for her cue to enter. Thankfully, Fiona had ignored her request for a black wedding dress. C.C. knew she was being overly dramatic. She should relax and enjoy the moment. She should think of this as a dress rehearsal for the day when she really did marry her Prince Charming.

Most brides took months or even a year or more to plan for their wedding. The preparations for hers had taken mere hours. Maybe taking less time wasn't such a bad thing: less time for second thoughts.

Guests continued to file into the ballroom, which had been transformed into the perfect setting for a wedding. There were so many flowers C.C. thought the sisters must have emptied all the flower shops in Inverness.

The Victorian wedding dress fit her as though it had been made for her. She thought of her family and wished they could be here, even if it was a sham wedding. Her sisters would have been weepy, her brother would have snapped a zillion photos, and her father would have walked her down the aisle.

She'd purposely waited until a few minutes ago to call them and leave a message, knowing that with the nine-hour time difference they'd be asleep. She'd debated about calling them at all, but she had to at least let them know what had happened before the news broke all over the world that an unknown had married the football star Michael Campbell.

By the time her siblings woke up, the wedding would be over. They'd be upset, and she didn't blame them. This was the moment when a bride should feel the most like a princess and be able to bask in the love of family and friends. A lump caught in her throat.

William stepped over to her. He wore a formal black tuxedo with tails and had trimmed his salt-and-pepper beard to shape his face. The resulting look was very Sean Conneryish.

When he reached her side, he made a slight bow and smiled. "Never in my life have I seen a bonnier bride." C.C. nodded a thank you, too nervous to respond. The smile lines at the corners of his eyes crinkled together as he held out his arm. "If this be a proper wedding, the bride should not walk down the aisle alone. Would you do me the honor?"

She thought she'd convinced herself that it didn't matter that her family wasn't here. She knew that thought had been a lie from the beginning. William was offering to stand in for her father. A kind gesture that only made her miss her family more. She accepted his offer, and whispered, "Thank you."

His eyes twinkled as he rested his hand over hers. "I caught a glimpse of Miss Tatiana and her mum. Neither looked too pleased. They both looked like they were chewing on mouthfuls of angry wasps."

Her tension eased a little as C.C. pictured them. "Thank you for the image," she said, squeezing his hand. "But I thought this was Tatiana's idea?"

"It was," William said with a smile. "Before, that is, she saw you in your wedding dress."

The notion that someone like Tatiana might be jealous was unthinkable. If true, however, C.C. realized that she may have misjudged her. Could it be that even Tatiana was insecure? Or was her reaction part of the role they were supposed to play? She wanted to believe it was all an act. After all, Tatiana and Michael were engaged. There was no reason for her to be jealous "Please can we change the subject? All brides are beautiful on their wedding day."

William squeezed her hand. "Perhaps."

"You look very handsome, by the way."

His glance slid over to where Lady Roselyn stood giving final instructions to the caterers. "I hope you are not the only one who noticed. Expect the unexpected, my late wife would say, and life will always be filled with magic and miracles."

"Promise?"

"Promise." He bent his head down. The lines across his forehead deepened. "You are trembling like a butterfly caught in a net," he said.

"That sounds about right." She swallowed down the lump in her throat. "I know this isn't real. I know Michael and I are pretending we're in love so he can announce to the world that he has settled down with a wife. Tomorrow when I wake up, Michael will have secured his movie deal, and then after *Highland Rebel* is released we will let the press know it was all a mistake." Her laugh sounded hollow in her ears as she lifted the white-rose-and-lavender bouquet to her nose as her vision blurred. "I just wish the sisters hadn't made me look like a completely different person. I didn't recognize myself when I looked in the mirror. I'm sure that's what surprised Tatiana, as well. And how did they do everything so fast? The wedding decorations are lovely, my dress is a dream come true, the flowers..."

William handed her his handkerchief. "Michael told me that if you want to back out of the marriage, he'll give you the bonus you need either way."

She dabbed at her eyes, careful not to smudge her makeup. Everyone had gone to a lot of trouble to transform the ugly duckling into a swan, and now, before she even walked down the aisle, she was going to make a mess of their efforts. But she couldn't stop her thoughts. All her life she'd dreamed of a wedding like this one, but in the dream she was marrying someone who was crazy in love with her. Nowhere in her dreams was the marriage a business proposition.

She handed William's handkerchief back to him. *Get a grip. Michael has been very generous.* Because of him, she would be able to take care of her father, with enough money left over to start her business. She'd woken this morning feeling as though a cloud were following her. *Expect the unexpected.* She liked that expression. It sure fit today. She'd had an emotional breakdown, and if she didn't stop the tears before they had a chance to flow, her makeup would streak. Instead of a princess, she'd look like the bride of Frankenstein.

She straightened. "Yes, Michael told me that he'd give me the bonus, regardless, but I can't just take his money when I think this plan will help him. If only he hadn't put himself in this situation in the first place. He needs this marriage to prove to the world that he is no longer a...a..."

"A Scottish *hallirackit*?"

C.C. tilted her head. "I'm not sure what that means."

"It means a lad who is wild, rowdy, and irresponsible."

C.C. smiled for the first time in what seemed like decades. "I was going to say 'spoiled child,' but that is perfect. The Scots have great words."

"Aye, that we do."

The double doors to the ballroom swung open. "Are you ready?" William said.

"If I'm being honest, I'm far from being ready. But I've decided to take your advice and expect the unexpected."

Chapter Ten

Michael took his place beside Harold at the end of the ballroom. Chairs covered in white satin were arranged neatly in rows on each side, creating an aisle for the bride. Sprigs of white lavender and bouquets of blush pink rosebuds crowded every available space. He had to hand it to Harold and the sisters for pulling together a wedding on such short notice. Finding so many roses in the dead of winter had to be a Herculean feat all on its own. Not to mention finding so many people willing to attend a wedding on New Year's for complete strangers.

When he first signed on to Harold's crazy Hail Mary play, Michael had called his nana. The last thing he wanted was for his grandmother to be blindsided with news that her only grandson was getting married. Even with the nine-hour time difference, he knew she'd be awake. Ever since he'd started traveling, she had adjusted her schedule to fit his. She said she never wanted to be asleep when he called.

His grandmother had accepted the news as he expected. In fact, she'd wanted to hop on a plane as soon as he'd told her. He'd had to then break it to her that it wasn't a real wedding. It was all for show. The silence on the other end of the line had been deafening. She disapproved of deception of any kind. He'd felt her disapproval as though she were standing next to him with her hands perched on her hips and her frown deepening. That was, until he'd told her it was C.C. he was marrying and not Tatiana. Then she'd asked the strangest question.

"This turned out better than I hoped," Harold said, interrupting Michael's train of thought. "The press is here and lapping it up. I'm not sure where the sisters got all the guests, but it's a nice touch. Did Tatiana like the ruby necklace I bought for you to give her? They're her birthstone."

"She threw a lamp at me."

"Did you make sure it was in a public place? I hate this deception."

"Yes, and I'm sure by now it's all over the news, just as planned."

Michael focused on the double doors where the bride was to make her entrance. He wasn't surprised by Harold's response. His best friend had a soft heart. He always thought the best of everyone, even Tatiana. It was this outlook that had first drawn Michael's attention when he'd saved him from the bullies in grammar school. Michael had wanted to pummel the guys who'd hurt his friend. Harold had told him to let them go with a warning. And he had.

"Who'd you hire to play the part of the priest?" Michael said. "This guy looks like the real deal."

"Father John is the real deal. If the press found out we used an actor, our story would fall apart faster than a house of cards. Don't look so shocked. You know hiring a genuine priest was our only call."

"Did you tell C.C.?"

Harold glanced toward the double doors at the end of the ballroom. "Under the circumstances, I thought it unwise, and with Tatiana and her mother acting weird, we can't take any chances."

"What do you mean 'weird'?"

"They're having second thoughts."

"This was their idea."

Harold tried to loosen his collar but gave up. "That was before they saw C.C. in her wedding dress. I caught a glimpse of her when I came in. Time for game faces. It's starting."

The double doors opened, and a harpist began to play. C.C. appeared on the threshold, her arm resting on William's.

"Wow," Harold said. He nodded to C.C. as she walked down the aisle beside William. "The sisters are miracle workers. C.C. actually looks gorgeous. Who knew that under all that hair and black clothing was a real-life beauty? No wonder Tatiana is jealous. The good news is that she should be able to pull off the next phase of the plan."

Michael narrowed his gaze. "What have you done?"

Harold shrugged. "Just a little performance, insurance by Tatiana to make sure this wedding makes it into the press. Now, don't look at me. You need to concentrate on your bride."

Michael adjusted his tie, squared his shoulders and turned toward C.C. as she walked down the aisle. For once he had to agree with his friend. C.C. looked like a goddess. He knew now without a shadow of a doubt that this plan had been a mistake, but not for the reasons everyone seemed to think. What had he gotten himself into? Michael moved closer to the priest, keeping his focus on C.C. Her white dress clung to her body and glittered with crystals and pearls. Her hair was swept back from her face, and makeup highlighted her eyes.

He loved her eyes. They were what he'd noticed about her when they first met. He'd learned to tell the mood she was in by studying their shade. On most days they were light brown. When she was frustrated with him, which was often, her eye color would darken to the color of cinnamon with specks of red highlights. His favorite so far was when he'd seen her talking to Nana when she'd come for a visit at Christmas. The shade had been a warm caramel. He wondered what they looked like when she was kissed.

He shook himself and refocused. She was halfway down the aisle. Now he was the idiot. What was he doing? He didn't deserve a person like C.C. It didn't matter that this was a fake wedding. Guys like him didn't marry women like C.C. He should have asked Tatiana to stop wasting time and sign her divorce papers so they could be married. The world would have believed that match.

"Hey, pal," Harold said. "Are you all right?"

"Peachy."

The music softened and then faded away as C.C. reached his side. He searched her eyes, but the color kept changing. He wasn't sure if that was a good sign or a bad one.

She held out her hand. "Hi."

Her simple word released the breath he'd been holding. "Hi."

Chapter Eleven

C.C. put her hand in his. Her analytical side rationalized that because she could balance her checking account and do her own taxes, it meant she could do this without swooning over the fact that he had big hands. They enveloped hers as though hers belonged to a child, not a grown woman. Of course he had big hands. He was a quarterback. They needed big hands. Her analytical side might be calm, but her emotional side was in a runaway car headed for a cliff.

But it wasn't just that. She was used to seeing Michael in his football uniform, or when he was working out in the gym, or going out with Tatiana. In all those situations where they interacted it was easy to keep her focus on business. That he was good-looking was an understatement. For starters, although the rest of the wedding party wore tuxedos, Michael wore a kilt, with his clan colors of dark green and black tartan with yellow and white contrasting threads. What was it about men in kilts? He looked even handsomer, which she hadn't thought possible. But he was the client and treated her like one of the guys. The perfect arrangement.

Even more puzzling than her jumbled emotions was that she'd felt a shift in how Michael was looking at her.

Her face warmed as she tore her gaze from his and

focused on the actor who was portraying the priest. The slender man introduced himself as Father John, and raised his voice to ask everyone, except the bride and groom, of course, to be seated.

There was a shuffling of chairs as everyone took their seats, with a little added whispering amongst themselves. When everyone settled down, the priest opened his book.

****

The ceremony was a blur. They'd opted out of a mass, going straight to the reciting of the vows. The next words after, "I now pronounce you husband and wife," brought C.C. crashing back to the present.

"Michael Campbell," Father John said, "you may kiss the bride."

C.C. cast a sidelong glance toward her groom. Correction. Pretend husband. He looked as stunned as she felt. Neither of them had discussed this part with anyone. If they had been friends, they might have been able to fake it, or at least giggle their way through. But they had a professional relationship and, except for the one time, they had never even been alone together. If they kissed, everyone, most importantly the press, would sense how awkward they were around each other.

Father John cleared his throat and whispered, "Everyone is watching."

Michael nodded to the priest, and the man stepped back, giving them space. Then Michael turned to face her, leaning forward and whispering so low she knew only she could hear. His breath was warm and feather soft against her skin. "I can tell them we don't kiss in public."

51

She tilted her head to meet his gaze. "Seriously? When have public displays of affection ever stopped you?"

He winced. "Point taken."

"And if we don't tell them something like that," she continued, "they'll know this is a sham marriage the moment we try to kiss each other."

He paused. "I have an idea. When was the last time someone's kiss made your toes curl?"

She moistened her lips. "Eighth grade," she said without hesitation. "I had a huge crush on Tommy Shepard. He, of course, didn't know I existed. We were at a party together, in a large group playing spin the bottle. When it was my turn, I spun the bottle and it pointed to Tommy. I was really surprised. He didn't hesitate. He came over and kissed me."

"I'm not surprised."

The priest cleared his throat and stepped toward them, an eyebrow raised. "Is there a problem?"

Michael shook his head and reached for both of C.C.'s hands. "Pretend I'm Tommy."

"Will you pretend I'm Tatiana?"

He leaned in closer. "I have someone else in mind."

His mouth pressed against hers. The sudden contact had a domino effect, setting every nerve in her body tingling. His hands moved up her bare arms. Tommy's had been a boy's kiss. Michael's was a man's. Her lips parted as she leaned in and the kiss deepened.

Tatiana slammed open the double doors to the ballroom. They banged against the walls. C.C. pulled away from Michael, but he kept hold of her hands as

Tatiana stormed down the aisle.

Tatiana's raven-dark hair floated around her shoulders, her makeup was flawless, and the skin-tight crimson designer dress was worthy of the red carpet. The entrance scene of the jilted lover couldn't have been scripted better. In her wake, a man with puffy red cheeks and a wide-lens camera scurried behind her, snapping pictures of the startled guests. He looked like the stereotypical over-zealous paparazzi.

True to character, Tatiana paused halfway down, giving everyone in the ballroom ample time for a clear view. She pointed toward Michael and C.C. and shouted, "I object!"

"Wrong storyline," Michael said under his breath. "This is not a courtroom. What was Harold thinking?"

Tatiana's four-inch heels clattered on the wood floor, drowning out the rapid beat of C.C.'s heart. Harold had briefed her that this might happen, but Tatiana's performance seemed over the top, even for her. Despite Michael trying to make light of the situation, C.C. knew Tatiana could ruin everything.

She reached Michael and C.C. and curled her manicured fingers into talons. "How long has this been going on behind my back? I will scratch out your eyes! See if he likes you then!"

The first thing that registered to C.C. was that Tatiana didn't look as though she were acting. The second was that Michael still held her hands. Was it for show?

Michael stepped between C.C. and Tatiana. "That's enough. We talked about this."

Tatiana drew closer, bringing with her the sharp smell of her perfume. Her long lashes lowered over her eyes and when they rose, her gaze was piercing. Her voice low so only those just in front of her could hear, she warned, "You'd better keep your promise. I know all your secrets."

The paparazzi snapped a series of pictures as the hum of conversation rose over the guests. He rushed toward the wedding couple and shoved a mic toward Michael.

"Is it true that your deceased father was an accused felon?"

Fiona, Bridget, and Lady Roselyn stepped in and led Michael and C.C. out a side door. "We need to get you as far away from here as possible," Fiona said.

Chapter Twelve

Michael could run but he couldn't hide.

His grandmother had repeated that saying over and over that first year when he'd learned the identity of his parents. He'd disagreed with her then, and until now he'd done a pretty good job of staying at least two steps ahead of the mountain of secrets and half-truths.

Lady Roselyn and her two sisters led him, C.C., and Harold into a strange room that was wall-to-wall doors of every size, shape, design, and color. Some were modern, but most of them looked as though they'd been plucked from the pages of history books.

"That went well," Harold said with a sarcastic tone in his voice as he loosened his tie. "Tatiana won't like that the reporters turned the spotlight on your past and ignored her performance. My guess is that she and her mother are attempting to regain control of the story."

"It won't work."

"Not so sure. What I do know is that we need more time. We can't let you make a statement until news of your marriage has had a chance to reach your fans and the studio heads. People love a wedding story. Especially one that catches them by surprise. Unfortunately, we're dealing with a time change. It's three in the morning in the States. If I'd thought this through, I'd have planned a fake honeymoon and hired a helicopter to whisk the two of you away tonight. But even if I had, the weather has turned too dangerous to fly."

"Excuse me," Fiona said. "I didn't mean to eavesdrop, but if you need a place to escape for a while, we may have a solution."

Bridget frowned. "Fiona. We can't... Lady Roselyn, please tell her what she's suggesting is not possible. We're not ready."

Fiona crossed her arms over her chest. "When did you become so afraid to take chances?"

Lady Roselyn stepped between the two women. "Ladies, please. I'm sure Harold has it under control."

"I wish it were under control," Harold said. "They smell a story, and they won't stop until they have an interview. I'm guessing they have the whole town, the train station, and even this mansion under surveillance. No one is going anywhere. So, unless you have a black hole that can transport Michael and C.C. to another dimension in time and space, our only hope is to try and give Tatiana a chance to distract them while we prepare a statement."

"Or," Fiona began, "we can send C.C. and Michael someplace where no one will be able to follow them, let alone guess where they've gone. It might give you the time you need."

"I know you're trying to help," Harold said, "but like I said, the reporters have the town locked up." He checked his watch. "Everyone stay here. I'll go to work preparing a statement."

When he'd left the room, Lady Roselyn turned to Fiona. "Absolutely not."

"But it is the perfect solution. Bridget! A little help. You have to agree this solution is the best way to keep them safe from the reporters."

Bridget nodded. "Fiona has a point."

Lady Roselyn threw up her hands. "When the two of you start agreeing on anything, that's when I start to worry. We did not discuss this. All we agreed to was hosting a wedding. Which we did. There was no discussion of...of..." She lowered her voice. "You know."

"I don't know why you're so resistant," Fiona said. "It's the perfect solution. Harold said he needed more time to develop a statement and allow Michael's fans to learn of the wedding. And since most of his fans are in the United States, and right now it's about nine o'clock in the morning on the East Coast, and even earlier in the rest of the country, my option is not only perfect, it may be the only one we have."

"You planned this from the beginning," Lady Roselyn said.

Fiona was the picture of innocence. "I have no idea what you're talking about."

"Then it's decided," Bridget said.

"I'm lost," C.C. said. "What is everyone talking about?"

"Go ahead, Fiona," Lady Roselyn said. "Tell them. After all, this was your idea. I suppose you've chosen a date."

"December 31, seventeen hundred forty-five."

"Excellent choice," Bridget said. "Inverness in that century, particularly around the Scottish New Year of Hogmanay, is magical. Speaking of magic, I'd better make sure our New Year's celebration in this century meets our guests' expectations."

Lady Roselyn rubbed the bridge of her nose. "The

two of you have lost your minds."

Fiona ignored her and turned to C.C. and Michael. "While Bridget tends to our guests, I'll fill you in on a few details. Have the two of you ever wanted to time travel?"

Chapter Thirteen

While Fiona sat down with C.C. and Michael to explain what would happen to them, Lady Roselyn decided it best to stay out of the way.

The room Lady Roselyn referred to as the Door Room was the size of a basketball gymnasium. Green velvet drapes, trimmed in gold, shrouded the windows looking out on the riverside, while doors covered the other three walls. The first thing a person might notice was that there seemed to be more doors than normal, as though you had dropped down Alice in Wonderland's rabbit hole. There were dozens of doors in various sizes and shapes. And just as in Alice's story, it mattered which door you chose. One door could lead to a leisurely walk in Victorian England, while another might lead you to the battlefields of Napoleon's Waterloo.

Lady Roselyn and Fiona had told Michael and C.C. they would send them some place safe from the reporters, and sending them back in time would certainly accomplish that promise.

William had installed an ample supply of doors in case couples attending the New Year's Eve party wanted to sample some of the adventures the sisters offered. The matchmakers were responsible for uniting many of the happy couples in attendance, so this was more than just a New Year's Eve party: it was a reunion. Lady Roselyn liked to imagine that she and her sisters were like Rick Steves, the travel guide who had introduced thousands of Americans to Europe through his European tours, whereas the sisters used their adventures to awaken couples to the possibility of love.

Fiona was briefing Michael and Bridget on what to expect. If the reaction of couples they'd dealt with in the past was any indication, Michael and C.C. wouldn't believe they'd traveled back in time until they experienced it for themselves.

Lady Roselyn had tried to stay upset with Fiona, but she couldn't. In fact, if she were honest, a big part of her was pleased. She doubted few guests at the wedding had missed the way C.C. and Michael had looked at each other, or the sparks that had flown when they kissed. All the couple needed was the time to realize what most people already suspected: C.C. and Michael were falling in love. No, she wasn't upset with her sister. How could she be? After all, Fiona was doing what they'd been born to do. She was playing matchmaker.

William had finished installing the door marked with the year seventeen hundred forty-five, and he turned to join her. He cast a dashing figure, as the Victorians would say, and for some reason he looked much younger. It struck her that she wished he hadn't cut off his beard, or that his shoulders didn't look so broad in his tux, or that he could always sense when she needed a good laugh or a kind word. Most of all, she wished she did not look forward to seeing him every day and felt bereft when he was away on business.

She glanced away before William could read the naked expression in her eyes. Their relationship had to remain professional. She concentrated on C.C. and Michael. Michael was glancing out the window, his hands laced behind his back. C.C. was seated next to Fiona, alternating between nodding her head and shaking it from side to side. The couple was processing the information, most likely believing that Fiona was delusional. Good. At least they weren't hysterical. That reaction was the hardest to deal with.

Too soon she turned back to William. He smiled, and she felt the heat of a blush betray her. She willed her voice not to give any more of her emotions away. The matchmaker code they lived by was unyielding. It was modeled after Queen Victoria. Marriages were arranged. The one departure from the Queen's dictum was that affairs before marriage were allowed. If a spouse died, however, the surviving widow or widower could never remarry. It was no wonder there was a shortage of matchmakers these days.

William bowed, as though sensing her inner turmoil. Most considered his old-fashioned way of greeting, although romantic and gallant, part of the matchmaker experience. The truth was far more complicated.

He motioned to the door he'd installed. "Fiona said to use the door marked Inverness, Scotland, December thirty-first, seventeen hundred forty-five. As soon as you give us the word, Fiona and I will go through, followed by C.C. and Michael. I'll drive them by coach from Urquhart Castle to Inverness and the rendezvous location. Fiona will meet them there, introduce them to the city, and stress the importance of returning to the rendezvous spot at the appropriate time. There's a large New Year's Eve celebration, or Hogmanay, as the Scots say, which should keep Michael and C.C. entertained while you, Bridget, and Harold keep the reporters distracted."

"Curious. When exactly did Fiona ask you to install this particular door?"

"This morning, shortly after Michael proposed the fake marriage to C.C."

Lady Roselyn looked over at her sister. Fiona's gift was sensing a couple's attraction to one another, long before they realized it themselves. "New Year's Eve in Inverness will be a magical time," she said to William. "The perfect setting for love to bloom. My sister has uncanny instincts."

"That she does."

What went unspoken was the turmoil in Fiona's own love life.

But Lady Roselyn knew that her sister understood Scotland's history, its pleasures as well as its dangers, and for C.C. and Michael it must be like listening to a tour guide who had actually been present at the events Fiona described. Lady Roselyn edged closer to listen.

"A large swath of Scotland's history," Fiona was saying, "has been plagued by the Jacobite rebellion. The effort to return the Stuarts to the throne of England tore Scotland and England apart. That France harbored King James and his descendants only increased the tensions between the two countries. But in December of seventeen hundred forty-five, there was a lull in the fighting, and Bonnie Prince Charlie used that time in Inverness to plan his next—and what was to be his last—battle, the one on the bloody field of Culloden."

At the mentioned of that battle, Lady Roselyn walked over to the door that was a match for one that had been on a cottage on the site of Culloden. The door was handcarved and pitted with bullet holes and burn marks. It was always the first door William installed. She pressed her hand against the wood, remembering the fallen men, before returning to the door that C.C. and Michael would use. Unlike the Culloden door, this wood door was more finely made and had the image of a Scottish thistle painted on its surface. Its mirror likeness hung in one of the few towers that remained at Urquhart Castle.

She unhooked a set of keys from the belt loop at her waist. "Our adventures don't always work," she said to William.

William was silent, perhaps remembering the same incident she had. "Should I tell Fiona that we've changed our minds?"

Lady Roselyn shook her head, banishing her concerns. She didn't doubt her sister's instincts. That was never in question. Fiona had taken an interest in this couple, which could be a sign that she respected her commitment to the matchmakers' family business. Another positive. But what to do about Liam? If Fiona didn't honor her betrothal to him...

"Are you sure Fiona insisted we use the door at the castle? The one in the Water Horse, er, the Matchmaker Café in Inverness has easier access. There must be a match between the door in our time and the one in the past for the enchantment to work."

"Your sister was most insistent," William said. "Fiona wouldn't even let me install another door as a backup in case the one at the castle couldn't be reached in time. The closest one we have installed to Inverness is the cottage door at Culloden."

"Fiona is a risk taker," Lady Roselyn said, selecting the key that would open the door. "One day I fear she may go too far."

"She mentioned that our couples needed to experience real conflict and danger. Only then will they realize whether or not they are suited for one another."

"She forgets that our couple is running from reporters, not seeking true love." When William answered her with just a shrug of his shoulders she heaved a sigh. She took in a deep breath and slipped the key into the lock. "Very well. Let Fiona know we are ready."

Chapter Fourteen

C.C. decided she must be dreaming as she snuggled under the warmth of a comforter, imagining she was on a ship, rocking slowly back and forth with the currents. It was the good kind of dream where the handsome prince had declared her the fairest in the land.

But she could feel the threads of the dream slipping through her grasp. The images became less clear, and she knew the moment she opened her eyes they would disappear. She squeezed her eyes tighter as she tried to hold onto her dream. She remembered exchanging vows with the prince, and a magical kiss that had made her toes curl. There was a fairy godmother who looked a lot like the café owner, Lady Roselyn. The fairy godmother and her sisters had announced that C.C. and her prince not only had to travel back in time but must return at the stroke of midnight or remain in the past forever. She'd then opened a door and escorted C.C. and Michael to a coach driven by six white horses.

C.C. sighed. Her parents would have loved the idea of their daughter fleeing with a handsome prince to a mysterious location in Scotland. Her whole childhood had been filled with such stories. She and her brother and sisters were taken to fairytale-themed movies, and their bookshelves at home had been filled with stories of enchanted princesses and knights in shining armor.

They'd even made summer pilgrimages to Oregon's Shakespeare Festival in Ashland. While most children had been playing games, she and her siblings wielded wooden swords or tanned leather. Her parents had even named their daughters after fairytale heroines— Cinderella, Briar Rose, from *Sleeping Beauty*, and Belle, from *Beauty and the Beast*—and their son, Galahad, after one of the knights of the Round Table.

The gentle rocking came to an abrupt halt, and C.C. slid off the bench seat and onto the floor of the coach with a thud. Her eyes snapped open. Michael rushed from the seat opposite hers, kneeling down in the cramped space, and helped her back to her seat. He was still wearing the dress kilt he'd worn at the wedding, and she was still in her wedding gown.

"It wasn't a dream," she said more to herself than to Michael.

"Would you rather it had been?" The intensity of his gaze quickened her pulse.

"I'm not sure," she said.

The door to the coach opened wide, and cold air blew inside. "We've reached our destination," William said. "Remember, and this is very important: you must return to Urquhart Castle by midnight tonight. The door you came through will be open, and that is the only way back to your own time. Fiona came through earlier and is here to both guide you and make sure you enjoy your adventure."

Michael jumped down from the coach and turned to help C.C. He seemed to be taking it all in stride, which was somewhat annoying. Or maybe he didn't believe time travel was possible any more than she did and was just playing along. She slipped her hand into his, and he helped her to the ground. Yes, that was it. No need to panic. As though to quiet her concerns, a short distance away were flickering lights, which C.C. assumed was the town of Inverness. It all looked perfectly normal.

Bridget had given her a fur-lined cap that had seemed too much when she was inside the mansion. Now she wished she hadn't turned down the boots, hat, and fur muff that were also offered. She felt like a leaf that had been swept down the currents of a fast-moving stream. First, there had been the wedding, and then the announcement that the only way to escape the reporters was to travel back in time. In the back of her mind, she had rationalized that the sisters were speaking in some sort of code, that traveling back in time meant going to another wing of the mansion, or taking a boat ride to a castle ruin. She glanced over at the lights again. Shouldn't there be more of them this time of night?

William tipped his hat to them. "Donna forget. Ye'll need to meet me back here at the appropriate time. We'll no' make it back in time if ye don't." He climbed back into the driver's seat, snapped the reins over the horse's rump, and sped back in the direction from which they'd come.

"William left us. And was it my imagination, or was his Scottish brogue thicker?"

Michael turned from watching the departing coach and scanned the path that looked as though it led to the town. "Maybe he's in character. We'll be fine. I think this is the way we should go."

"What do you mean you think? Don't you know?"

****

The mist clung to the town of Inverness as it lay

before her like a mythical kingdom. Gone were the harsh lights and tacky storefronts advertising plastic toy images of the Loch Ness Monster and bobble-headed doll likenesses of William Wallace. The River Ness rolled like liquid ebony on one side and the bonfires illuminated the city on the other as it prepared for New Year's Eve. Revelers packed the narrow streets. Vendors had set up their booths. She admitted that the town looked different from what she remembered, but perhaps they'd walked to a section of the city where, in honor of New Year's, the town had recreated the past. She liked the logic. Actually, any little scrap of logic sounded pretty good to her right now.

"Wait up," she said, rushing to catch Michael. "So you don't believe we traveled back in time?"

"I didn't say that. Actually it's the opposite. I'm convinced we did. In the twenty-first century there was a castle over on that hill. The locals called it a Victorian Folly. It's no longer there. Plus, I haven't seen a car or taxi."

"But you said we'd be fine."

"And you said I was Prince Charming. People say a lot of things when they don't think anyone is listening."

"I never said you were..." Her face heated into a blush. "Was I talking in my sleep?" When he nodded, she groaned. "I was delirious. That still doesn't explain why you think we'll be fine."

"No one has ambushed us yet."

She stubbed her toe and limped after him. "I don't think I like you very much."

"Follow me." Fiona seemed to materialize from the mist.

Startled, C.C. bumped into Michael. "Where'd you come from?"

"Liam and I arrived a short time before you, so we could make sure things were ready. Watch your step. A half a dozen or more sheep passed by here a short time ago." She seemed satisfied her words of warning were heard when C.C. and Michael stepped over a pile of steaming poo.

"Who's Liam?" C.C. said to Michael.

"Haven't a clue."

Fiona headed down a gentle path, speaking over her shoulder. "Bridget told me before I left that our guests were still talking about your kiss and the way Michael couldn't keep his eyes off his bride all through the ceremony. You both fooled everyone into believing that the two of you were madly in love. I wasn't fooled. I saw how you looked at each other the first time I saw you together."

"Who's Liam?" Michael said, interrupting.

"Liam and I are betrothed. More of an arranged marriage than a love match. Ironic. Matchmaker who doesn't marry for love." She whacked at a bush along the path with the back of her hand.

"Now that we're away from the mansion and the reporters," C.C. began, "you can tell us the truth. We didn't really time travel back to the eighteenth century, did we?"

Fiona glanced over her shoulder again. "You don't have to believe me. You'll see for yourself soon enough when we reach the town. William said you both had a nice rest on the coach. Most of our travelers feel disoriented or at least sleepy. Time travel takes a little getting used to. What you're experiencing is a lot like jet lag after a long flight. Very normal." She paused to face them. "If you are still sleepy, we have hotel rooms booked in town. Separate rooms, of course."

Michael blew on his hands, turning to C.C. "Are you tired?"

C.C. shook her head as she brought her cloak closer around her.

He nodded and spoke for both of them. "We're good."

"Perfect," Fiona said, resuming her way down the path. "When we reach the bottom of the trail I'll head you in the direction of the hotel, but if you'd rather explore the town, you're more than welcome to do that instead. As I was saying, there's nothing to worry about. We do this sort of thing all the time. Well, maybe not the part of inviting couples to hide out in the past. That's new. But the whole plan of traveling back in time is sort of our thing. Usually we have a little more time to prepare, but you'll be all right. There's nothing to worry about."

Chapter Fifteen

Michael was glad Fiona had left C.C. and him alone to explore the city. Fiona was too observant. No wonder she was in the matchmaking business. But he would have to be more careful. Had Tatiana also noticed his reaction to C.C.? Was that the reason for her overreaction?

He paused along the trail to the city to gain his bearings. He was an expert at locking down his emotions except when he was around C.C. She was different from the women he had dated. The first thing he'd noticed was that she listened, and the second was that her emotions were guarded. He knew she tried to make him smile or at least show some response. It was better if he kept things locked up. Yes, he had to be on his guard. Unlike his father, he'd survived. And he'd done it by keeping a check on his emotions. No extremes. That was his mantra, and he'd made it into an art form.

He relished the idea that no one knew what he was thinking. The women he dated alternated between liking that he was disconnected, which meant they didn't have to pretend they loved him for anything other than his money and fame, and those who wanted more. Tatiana appeared to fit both categories. He didn't mind, or at least he'd made peace with the fact that Tatiana had first been attracted to his celebrity and

71

wealth. That was part of who he was these days. But now he was tired of being alone.

The fake marriage idea had been Tatiana's, including choosing C.C. as the bride. He knew Tatiana hadn't seen C.C. as a rival. The marriage would help Tatiana in her divorce negotiations. Tatiana's husband was a quarterback for a rival team, and he'd made it clear he wasn't going to negotiate their prenuptial agreement if his wife was dating and possibly going to marry another football player, especially if that player were Michael Campbell. Tatiana was relying on the fact that she could play the sympathy card as the jilted girlfriend and gain the upper hand in the negotiations.

"Can we walk a little slower?" C.C. said, breaking into Michael's thoughts. "These shoes are beautiful, but they aren't made for speed walking."

Michael paused, gave a slight nod and turned, then wished he hadn't. C.C. was a vision. She was bathed in the glow of the streetlamps. Her hair had come loose, her face was flushed, and her lips were parted. She looked so kissable. He clenched his hands at his sides. How would she react if he tried to kiss her?

He'd known he liked being around her. Everything could be falling apart, but somehow she remained calm. Being near her reminded him of the time in the South when he and his team had been on a road trip after a hurricane had struck, and they had driven through the aftermath. All around them was chaos, but for a few brief miles it had been calm and serene, untouched by the storm for whatever reason.

The kiss they had shared at the ceremony had surprised them both. He could tell by her reaction. But was it the magic of the moment, or something else? If he tried to kiss her again, would she kiss him back? What was he thinking? Soon after they returned, they'd file for an annulment, and when Tatiana's divorce became final, he and Tatiana would be married. Tatiana had it all planned out, from the dress she would wear to the appetizers they would serve. He needed to face reality. C.C. was not for him.

He remembered he was still walking too fast and slowed down, resisting the urge to apologize. It was better if she thought he was an insensitive jerk. That was the role he'd heard his dad said all men had been born to play. Although why he should follow his father's advice he wasn't quite sure.

****

By C.C.'s calculation, it was around six o'clock in the evening, and this far north, it was already dark. The crescent moon, stars, and street lamps helped light the way along the wooden sidewalks. On the hill overlooking the town were rings of bonfires, the hill where in the nineteenth century, as Michael had said, the Victorian Folly would be built.

Markets hugged one side of the street, reminding C.C. of the Christmas marts she'd only seen from her limo when she first arrived in Inverness. Men, women, and children crowded into the streets, enjoying the New Year's Eve atmosphere. There were obvious differences in how the merchants dressed, and in the toys and ornaments—handmade versus machine-made—but the spirit of the holiday was the same.

Like modern-day markets, the vendors were grouped together along the River Ness according to categories. Just as in modern times, to accommodate hungry partygoers there were food venders, hawking everything from roasted chestnuts to dried meats and a variety of breads and almond pastries. On the other side of the street were the vendors that were more appealing to C.C.

There were tables with ornaments made from lace, handmade clothing, jewelry, jugglers, musicians, and a tall mime dressed as a court jester entertaining a group of laughing children and their parents.

C.C. dropped a few coins into the mime's donation cup. He came to life, taking off his jester's hat. The mime was well over six feet tall, with broad shoulders and a mischievous twinkle in his eyes. He made a sweeping bow and produced a bouquet of dried lavender. C.C. nodded her thanks and inhaled the rich fragrance. She nodded to the jester again and headed toward a booth where a young woman was selling clothing.

Michael stepped in front of her, blocking her path. "I know we decided to explore the town, but I'm thinking it would be wiser if we followed Fiona's advice and went to the hotel."

A couple passed by them, stared, and then whispered to each other before moving on.

C.C. glanced back at them and then quickly looked away, lowering her voice. "I think they overheard us talking. Didn't you say the English and Scots didn't like each other?"

"They hated each other, but it's seventeen forty-five, and the American Revolutionary War won't start until seventeen seventy-five. To the Scots, America is still a British colony. We have nothing to worry about. Our accents are probably only a curiosity to them. The good news is that it's December, and no one fights in the winter. There's a truce of sorts between England and Scotland. The English have retreated, and the Scots are busy taking care of their families for the winter. The Jacobite leader, Bonnie Prince Charlie, is holed up somewhere in Inverness waiting for better weather and planning what will be his final battle. The battle of Culloden won't be until April."

"What's the bad news?"

"I'm wearing the clan colors of a Campbell. They fought with the English and were considered traitors."

C.C. understood the implications, glancing around to see if she could tell whether or not anyone had noticed. If they had, would they look the other way because of the holiday, or would they consider Michael's choice to wear the Campbell's colors too bold a move to let pass? She cleared her throat. "You're welcome to check into the hotel, but, as I mentioned, I'm going shopping."

"But you don't shop."

"You don't know anything about me."

He seemed taken aback. "I mean, you're not like Tatiana. You're not interested in what you wear."

She eyed him for a few seconds, pleased that he winced under her stare. At least he had the good sense to realize he'd insulted her wardrobe choices. "Tatiana likes to shop. I've never seen her wear the same thing twice."

"Exactly. You're more practical."

For some reason his saying something that she normally would consider a positive rubbed her the wrong way. "You mean boring, bland, and quite uninteresting."

She knew she was baiting him, fishing to see what

he really thought of her. She'd always used the excuse that she didn't have time to shop for clothes. The truth was that she admired those who knew their style, their look. She, on the other hand, hadn't a clue about her style and often wondered if she even had one. She knew she didn't want to spare the money for a stylish wardrobe, though. As a result, her closet was filled with only one color: black. She reasoned that black was a professional color, a serious color. But most importantly she didn't have to worry about mixing and matching colors.

The mime reached out and handed her a paper rose. She wondered if he'd overheard the exchange between her and Michael. It seemed as though he wanted to say something but then changed his mind. She smiled a thank you to the mime and dropped another coin in his cup. Michael was still in stone-statue mode, perhaps trying to come up with a response to her statement. It didn't matter. She didn't know why she'd tried to get a human response from him in the first place. Better people than she was had tried and failed.

"I'm going shopping."

Chapter Sixteen

She'd been surprised when he joined her on her shopping spree. She knew he hated to shop. They'd visited most of the vendors along the River Ness, and she still hadn't found what she was looking for. But Michael Campbell wasn't the kind of guy who left a woman alone in a strange city. She'd discovered that when she interviewed for the job as Tatiana's assistant.

It had been late into the evening when her interview ended that day. Michael had asked how she planned to get back to her hotel, and she told him she was going to walk the eight blocks. Tatiana suggested C.C. take a taxi. Michael had insisted on walking her home. They hadn't spoken a word the entire time, and after he made sure she was safe in the lobby, he'd simply said good-bye and that he hoped she'd take the job as Tatiana's assistant.

C.C. had guessed that working for Tatiana would be a challenge. Tatiana had a reputation for being demanding, but C.C. admired the woman's work ethic. Tatiana had worked her way up from the assistant who helped dress the runway models to a runway model herself, and had started her own custom shoe empire. C.C. hoped that, in addition to the job and the needed income, she might also learn how to run a business from Tatiana.

Michael paused beside a jewelry vender and stood

examining the handmade rings. He hadn't said very much over the past hour. When she'd first seen him and Tatiana together this morning, they had been the picture of perfection. Two beautiful people who said all the right things about each other in public and seemed to sense the exact moment when someone would snap a picture. Sometimes, though, it was the things that weren't said or the times when they kissed and it looked more for show and photos than spontaneous passion that had C.C. wondering why they were together.

"If you don't mind my asking," Michael said, "what do the initials C.C. stand for?"

"Promise you won't laugh?"

"My middle name is Babe Ruth."

"What's wrong with that? You're named after the famous baseball player."

"I wish," Michael said. "Nana said that when my mother was pregnant she was addicted to Baby Ruth candy bars. She ate them morning, noon, and night. When I was born, she insisted on the modified name." He moved closer. "Your turn."

These days, the only time the question came up of what her initials stood for was when she had to sign a legal document. Her full name was on her passport, and she'd gotten plenty of raised eyebrows, but thankfully no one had ever made a comment.

She took a deep breath and plunged forward. "My father's last name is Charming, and when my parents married, they thought it would be fun to name their children after fairytale characters."

For a split second it looked almost as though Michael had started to smile. He caught himself, and frowned instead. "You're serious."

C.C. shrugged and strolled to the next vendor, who had a display of multi-colored ribbons that fluttered in the breeze. "Afraid so. My mother named me Cinderella, my sisters are Briar Rose and Belle, from *Sleeping Beauty* and *Beauty and the Beast*, and my brother is named Galahad, from *King Arthur and His Knights of the Round Table*."

"That's why you made such a sour expression when someone remarked that you were a modern-day Cinderella."

"Don't forget the shoes. Although it was generous of Tatiana to lend me a pair from her collection, they resemble the description of the glass slippers in the fairytale. But it's more than that. I think the Cinderella story misses the point. There's the fantasy that we can all fall in love at first sight or find our Prince Charming. Thousands of children have bought into that scenario. No one seems to wonder what happens to the couple the next morning. Do they still love each other in the cold light of day after all the lights, fancy clothes, and magic have disappeared? Or do they live to regret their decision?"

Michael fingered one of the ribbons hanging from the vendor's booth. "What was his name?"

C.C. reached for a pink ribbon and paused. "You're suggesting that someone broke my heart."

"Why else would you dislike a classic fairytale?"

"Are you telling me you believe in the nonsense of love at first sight?"

"Let's say I'm not ruling it out."

"Tommy Shepard."

Michael lifted an eyebrow. "The spin-the-bottle guy? He's the one who made you stop believing in love?"

"He's the one. It started out like a fairytale. We kissed, and he started planning our future after the first date. We even attended the same college, enrolled in the same classes. It felt a little too fast, even back then, but I thought this was the forever-after kind of love. Between my sophomore and junior year, my mother died. Tommy had taken an internship in D.C. I called and gave him the news, and told him when the services would be held. He said he couldn't leave his internship, but even if he could, he didn't like funerals."

"I'm not sure anyone does."

"Yes, well, he didn't stop there. He said, and I quote, 'Your family is weird and will make it a fairytale-themed funeral. If I attend, I'll risk my reputation,' end of quote."

"You broke up with him."

She smiled, liking that he'd guessed correctly. "I ended it right there and then."

"Good for you." He paused. "Did it?"

"Excuse me?"

"Did the funeral have a fairytale theme?"

She laughed softly, remembering her family's reaction to Tommy's words. "We'd planned the traditional funeral. After my conversation with Tommy, I called my family. They loved the idea of a themed funeral, and they agreed that our mother would have loved it, too. It felt right. We each dressed up in a costume that represented our character's names. We told our friends, and many of them also attended in costume. We laughed, and we cried. It was an amazing celebration of our mother's life."

"I wish I'd known you then."

"You would have come in costume?"

"Why would that be so strange? I dress up like a knight every time I step out on the football field. Helmet, pads that are like the early cloth armor worn before chainmail and metal, all that's missing is a sword and shield. Sometimes I think if some in the league had their way, we'd have those too."

"You surprise me. So you might have attended the funeral dressed like King Arthur."

"That would have been a high possibility. I blame Nana. She loved the happily-ever-after stuff and dragged me to her favorite romantic comedies and fairytale movies. The deal was that if I accompanied her so she wouldn't have to go alone, when I finished my homework, she'd let me watch sports on television. As a result, and I can't believe I'm admitting this, I have my own spin on the Cinderella story. I think she was brave. In order to go to the ball, she had to find the courage to step out of her comfort zone. She had to be able to take risks. She was going to the ball to meet the prince, but there were no guarantees he'd notice her. And although I agree that you should know a person well before you commit, you can also tell a lot about a person when you first meet. The prince may not have known for sure that they could make their marriage work, but he knew two things. He knew he needed to see her again, and he was willing to take a risk that it might not work out."

She shivered and pulled the cloak closer around her shoulders. "Do your fans know you're a Cinderella fan?"

"Nice deflection, Cinder Girl. You look cold." Michael sluffed off his coat and draped it over her shoulders.

"I can't feel my toes."

"Why didn't you say something sooner?"

She didn't want to tell him that she was having too much fun and didn't want it to end. "The coat helps, thank you."

"You were looking for boots. I should have known."

"There you go again, making me sound practical."

He swept her off her feet and into his arms. "I like practical. Besides, we're almost there."

She wrapped her arms around his neck, feeling as though she were dreaming again. *Hold on*, she cautioned. He might be a chivalrous knight, but he was Tatiana's chivalrous knight.

After half a block, he stopped under a wooden sign that hung from metal rings above a door: The Water Horse. She recognized the building. It was the site of the Matchmaker Café in the twenty-first century. Instead of a café, the sign indicated that this establishment was a tavern.

Chapter Seventeen

With C.C. still in his arms, Michael shouldered the door open. The stupidity of his gender never ceased to amaze him. Tommy Shepard had been a fool. So what if he might have had to wear a costume? C.C.'s mother had died. Families were everything. It didn't matter if you had dozens of family members or one or two. Families shared a bond that couldn't be broken.

A blast of warm air, the aroma of baking bread, and the hum of conversation welcomed him and C.C. into the crowded tavern. There had been few changes over the centuries. The same cheery fire crackled on the hearth, and a long trestle-style bar hugged the far wall.

Women in ankle-length skirts carried foaming tankards of ale or trays of brown bread and thick soup instead of lattes and pre-packaged pastries. As though to underscore the point that they were no longer in the twenty-first century, there wasn't an electronic device in sight.

Michael set C.C. down and reached for her hand as he led the way into the small, crowded room, looking for a vacant table. He found one near the fireplace, and as soon as they sat down a waitress appeared with a small wedge of shortbread.

"Fiona?" C.C. said. "What are you doing here?"

"Watching over the two of ye, of course," she said with a rich Scottish brogue. Michael noticed her accent was also thicker than he remembered, just like William's. Probably to allow them to blend in better with the locals. "Liam was keeping an eye on you," she continued, "and told me you were headed this way. The Water Horse is a fine choice. 'Tis one of the finest establishments in the city. My apologies for the wee bit of shortbread. Most of our cooks have taken off early to join the celebrations."

"We don't mind," C.C. said, breaking off a corner and passing the rest of the shortbread to Michael. "Who is Liam?"

"Why, he is the mime who was dressed as a jester. We make it a rule that when we send our guests back in time some of us join them to make sure they have a good experience."

C.C. took a nibble of her shortbread. "Why has the tavern been named the Water Horse?"

"In honor of the beastie that is guardian of the waters around Inverness. It's said he has never harmed a child, and in fact it's considered good luck if a child sees him. It's only around the holidays when there is a lot of noise and fireworks that he becomes ill-tempered and the water foams and froths like a witch's caldron. Hogmanay is the worst. He'll keep out of sight, for sure, but those foolish enough to venture out on Hogmanay have met with watery deaths."

Men at another table nearby called over to Fiona to bring them another round of ale and something to eat. They were richly dressed. Fiona nodded toward them, then turned back to C.C, lowering her voice. "You were wise to leave the mansion when you did. I've received word that the reporters have been turning our home upside down looking for you."

"Lass," one of the men from the neighboring table shouted. "Did ye not hear us? The prince and his men are thirsty."

"I'd best be moving along," Fiona said. "The prince is none other than Bonnie Prince Charlie himself. 'Twould be unwise to neglect royalty in these days and times."

Michael watched Fiona as she waited on the men. There were five in total. It was easy to pick out which one was the prince. He was dressed in bright colors: a peacock surrounded by mud hens. "I'm torn between asking the prince for his autograph or asking why he didn't march on London when he had the chance. If he had, historians believe he might have succeeded in controlling the city and regaining the crown for the Stuarts. Instead, he will be remembered as the man who would be king and the one responsible for the slaughter at Culloden."

"We should warn him that the battle will fail."

Michael drummed his fingers on the table. "We can't change history."

"Says who?"

"Scientists, writers, Star Trek…"

C.C. smiled. "You like fairytales, and you're a science nerd. What would your fans say? But conjecture regarding time travel aside, to my knowledge no one has actually traveled back in time."

"You're forgetting the matchmaking sisters. Don't you think if it were possible to change some of the horrific events in history they would have?"

"Lady Roselyn said they need the right door to travel to the time they want. Maybe they don't have the right ones for all situations." She leaned against the back of her chair. "It was just a thought. New topic. Do you think that really persistent reporter could have followed us here?"

Michael kept his gaze locked on the rolling flames in the fireplace. "I'm not worried about him anymore."

"Well, then why did we leave in the first place?"

"At the time it seemed important. I've been running from my past so long it has become a habit." His voice sounded strained and hard. "Now I'm not so sure it wasn't a waste of time." His voice trailed off, smothered by the clatter of plates and tankards of ale being delivered to customers. "There's something in my past I'd like to keep buried."

She folded her arms across her chest. "What do you think the reporter suspects?"

He turned toward her. "Nothing good."

"Nothing good, like you received a B in physics or skipped football practice, or nothing good as in you broke the law? I made it clear before I was hired that I will not be around people who have a wanton disregard for the law."

His mouth twitched up at the corner. "Yes, you made that quite clear during your interview. Do you know that you were the only person we interviewed who stressed that point? Your mother was a trial attorney, as I remember. And to answer your question, I've never so much as had a traffic ticket." He looked away, as though interested in the activity going on in the tavern. He could tell she wanted to press him. He wasn't ready.

Pots and pans crashed on the floor just outside the kitchen, followed by loud yelling. C.C. rose from the table. "Let's see if we can help Fiona."

Chapter Eighteen

C.C., with Michael close behind, headed toward the tavern's kitchen. She had never met a kitchen she didn't like. She supposed that was a strange thing to admit, even to herself. She guessed the reason she liked kitchens so much was because most of her fondest memories were of the times spent with her mother preparing meals. Together they would create new sandwiches to pack for her sisters' and brother's lunches. Most were a success. However, the chopped olives and the cold cooked asparagus sparked open rebellion. Her siblings threatened to eat cafeteria food if there was not one day a week where the sandwich was peanut butter with homemade strawberry or raspberry jam. Reluctantly, she and her mother agreed to their terms. Her mother considered cafeteria food unhealthy.

C.C. smiled at the memory as she shoved open the door and was hit with a wave of heat pulsating from the small kitchen. It looked much smaller than the one in the twenty-first century. It must have been remodeled and expanded over the centuries.

Fiona and only one other young woman were busy preparing food for the customers. The young woman's face was flushed as she loaded plates of bread and bowls of soup on her tray. She then hurried past C.C. and Michael so fast the braid she'd wound in a loose circle on top of her head, like an ebony crown, seemed likely to spring apart and uncoil.

Directly behind the table was a walk-in hearth that ran the length of the wall and rose to the ceiling. Flames churned and crackled around wood logs, pouring heat into the small room. Dried herbs hung from the beams alongside ropes of garlic and onions.

Fiona glanced up from ladling soup into a wooden bowl.

"We're here to help," C.C. said. "Put us to work."

Fiona's pinched expression softened with relief as she set the bowl on the table and rushed to give C.C. a hug. "We're saved. Molly and I didn't know how we were going to survive." She grinned. "We were afraid the crowd out in the tavern might turn ugly if we announced we were out of food. I should decline your offer," she chatted on in a rush. "You shouldn't be working here. You and Michael should be enjoying the celebrations."

"Not a chance," Michael said. "You're stuck with us."

C.C. grinned. "What he said."

Fiona shook her head. "I knew there was something I liked about you two."

"You lost your Scottish brogue," Michael said.

Fiona laughed. "You noticed." Her smile broadened. "Between you and me, it's sometimes exhausting." After handing C.C. a long white apron to help protect her dress, she gave Michael a tray filled with tankards of ale. "Molly will show you who placed these orders. This will give *you* a chance to practice your brogue." When Michael left, she turned back to C.C. "As I said, we are running out of food."

C.C. fitted the apron against her waist and wound

the ties around twice to secure it. She surveyed the kitchen. Fiona was right. The last of the lamb stew bubbled in an iron pot on the hearth. It had boiled down. Ale could be used to extend it a little. They might get as many as another dozen or so bowls. What they needed was innovative thinking.

C.C. started to take an inventory. Cooling in the larder was a round of cheese, what was left of a side of raw beef, and a full haunch of smoked ham. What they had in abundance was baked bread, cooling on racks. "I have an idea, but do you know when sandwiches were invented?"

"Sixteen sixty," Michael said as he reentered the kitchen, headed over to the keg, and filled tankards of ale from the spigot. "John Montague, the Fourth Earl of Sandwich, is credited with the idea. He wanted to keep his hands from touching the meat when he traveled." He loaded up his tray and headed toward the door.

C. C. and Fiona both glanced toward Michael as he disappeared back into the tavern, and then at each other. They both burst out laughing.

"He is like a walking, talking Wikipedia," Fiona said with a wide smile. "Is he always like that, or is this because he's researching Scottish history for the part he might play in the movie?"

C.C. shook her head. "This is classic Michael. He seems to love knowing random things most people would find boring. Once when we were at the café waiting for Tatiana and her mother, I asked him if he knew how the game of football started. An hour later I'd learned football was an early version of rugby that was played in Britain in the nineteenth century. Someone by the name of William 'Pudge' Heffelfinger started professional football in 1892, and in 1920 the American Professional Football Association was formed. There was a demonstration game at the 1922 World's Fair and a competition game at the 1932 summer Olympics." C.C. grinned. "There were a lot more dates and events, so many they had my mind spinning. Fortunately, Tatiana and her mother finally arrived."

"You like him."

"He and Tatiana are engaged."

"Ah. I'll change the topic. Why did you want to know the origin of a sandwich?"

"I wanted to make sure that sandwiches wouldn't seem odd. I have an idea of how we can stretch what is left of the food. We can make one of my mother's favorites: meatball sandwiches. We'll tell the customers it's special in celebration of Hogmanay. Sandwiches will help stretch the little meat we have left. I'll need someone's help grinding the beef. We will combine the mixture with garlic, onion, and herbs, and then form them into meatballs. When they're cooked, we will be back in business. Until they're ready, we'll serve up what is left of the soup, and make ham and cheese sandwiches."

"Does Michael know about your hidden talent?"

"Making sandwiches isn't that big a deal. Anyone can do it."

Fiona smiled. "I wasn't talking about making sandwiches, I was talking about the talent you have to recognize a problem and come up with a simple solution. That is rare."

Chapter Nineteen

C.C.'s sandwiches were a big hit. Michael was a short distance away, taking orders and serving customers. Nowhere in his bio did it list that he'd worked as a waiter, and yet he looked as though he'd had years of experience.

She approached Bonnie Prince Charlie's table. He and his men were laughing over a joke they'd shared. The prince sat back in his chair to watch her as she gave each man a plate of meatball sandwiches.

When she set the prince's order in front of him, he gave her a dazzling smile. He'd removed his wig. His hair was tied at the nape of his neck and his deep-set eyes were framed by long lashes. He ignored the constant chatter of his men, concentrating his attention on C.C. A slow smile spread across his features as he winked at her and reached out to grab her waist.

She swerved out of his grasp and headed to a table next to his. Michael had told her a little about his history. Bonnie Prince Charlie was a notorious playboy, and it was rumored that after he fled the battle of Culloden, a woman helped hide him from the English. The irony was that when he finally made his escape to France and exile, he had been dressed as a woman.

The prince caught her staring, lifted his wine glass, and toasted her. "If you're looking for a man, I'm yours, *mon chéri*."

Out of nowhere, Michael moved quickly to her side. "Leave her alone." Gone was the Scottish brogue he'd been practicing with customers. His voice was hard and monotone. "She's my wife."

"*Impossible*. If I had a wife as beautiful as yours, she'd not be here; she'd be in my bed."

The prince's comment drew laughter from his friends. The men all raised their tankards and clinked them together in agreement. The prince nodded to the man closest to him. The man had a wild beard that fanned out over his chest. He nodded back, drained his ale, wiped foam from his mouth onto his sleeve, then eased away from the table and stood.

He wasn't as broad-shouldered as Michael, but he was almost as tall. He smoothed down his beard. "The prince has taken a liking to your wife. Name your price."

Michael's expression darkened as he set his tray on a table. "The lady is not for sale," Michael shot back. His defiance of the prince brought a hush over those nearby.

The prince's expression froze in place, and his eyes went dark and cold.

The bearded man rested his hand over the hilt of his sword. "My prince will take this wench, if ye will it or no."

Muscles around Michael's jaw tightened as he balled his hands into fists and edged toward the man. "She's not merchandise that can be bought and sold. Apologize to my wife. Now."

Time seemed to hold its breath. The man hesitated. He seemed to be assessing Michael for the first time.

C.C. had told Michael once that he never showed

emotion. She had never understood the reason. She'd assumed it was because he was that rare athlete who could keep his feelings in check. He played with an intensity that few could match but never lost his temper, on or off the field. The moment the game was over, he had a standing rule. If any reporters wanted an interview, it was common knowledge they'd have to wait until Michael was ready. She'd assumed it was a power play, a way for Michael to exert his control over the media. What if it was something else? What if he needed time to calm down after a game and regain his control?

Watching Michael now, and the reaction of the men at the prince's table, she knew the outcome if a fight broke out. Once Michael was in motion, he was unstoppable. He always completed a pass, or if a receiver weren't in the pocket, he'd make the run himself. She'd said watching him play was boring, but that had been just an attempt to get a reaction from him.

Harold had said that when Michael was in high school he'd played both quarterback and defensive back, offense as well as defense. He didn't care what position he played as long as he was on the field of battle.

When Michael Campbell was on the field, he was anything but boring. No one could keep their eyes off him. He made things happen. His coaches were always yelling at him to stop taking chances, as he risked injuries by making the play himself. The coaches might as well have been talking to a statue, which was probably the reason the press referred to him as one. Someone in the press had written an article saying Michael reminded him of Auguste Rodin's bronze sculpture, *The Thinker*. The fact that Rodin wanted his sculpture to depict intellect as well as poetry and strength fit Michael Campbell perfectly.

Perhaps the prince's men sensed that Michael was not the type of man who backed down and gave better than he received and that was why they hesitated. Most men had a keen awareness of who was the alpha dog and where they fit in the pack.

The big bearded man had also been drinking, probably most of the day. She saw the shift in his decision. When he squared his shoulders, she knew he was counting on his friends to give him the advantage and backup he needed. Except they didn't look in any better shape than he did.

C.C. didn't feel in any danger, but they were in a strange place, and according to Fiona, the last thing they needed was to draw attention. She put her hand on Michael's arm. "We should go."

The bearded man put his hand over his heart as he drew closer. "Your wife's accent has a touch of the Sassenach. I have no love for the English, but when she speaks, I dinna care. Is your touch as soft as your voice, lassie? I'll have a go at you when the prince's had his fill. Ladies leave my bed with a smile on their face."

"That's it," Michael said through clenched teeth. He crossed the short distance, pulled back his fist, and hit the man in the jaw.

The man's head jerked to the side from the blow as he staggered back into his chair, sitting down hard. He rubbed his jaw and pushed himself back up, then paused. "He's wearing the clan plaid of those traitorous Campbells, lads. I didna notice that before."

The ebb and flow of conversation quieted as, one

by one, people turned toward Michael and C.C. She could feel the resentment rising in the room like steam. Men stood, chairs toppled, and drinks spilled.

Fiona had rushed to their side, pressing what looked like a plaid blanket into C.C.'s arms. "Take this," she said quickly. "It's a kilt in the old style but the only thing I could find. You should run."

They didn't need a second warning. Michael grabbed C.C.'s hand, and they headed toward the door.

Chapter Twenty

Once outside, Michael and C.C. ducked into a narrow alley just as the door of the Water Horse tavern slammed open and angry men poured out into the street. With C.C. at his side, Michael headed deeper into the shadows. Muffled shouts of revenge against the Campbells drifted farther and farther away as the men searched the town.

In the pitch black of the alley, Michael felt his way along the wall of the building on his left. It veered slightly around a corner and led to a garden illuminated by a star-studded night. How could he have been so stupid? He knew the history of the Campbells during this century. To say that they were disliked was an understatement. The sisters had a variety of kilts he could have chosen, but he'd wanted to wear his family's colors to impress C.C.

He glanced over at her. She'd bent down to pet a snow-white kitten that had been rubbing against her legs. Most people would be afraid of a cat that was most likely feral, but not C.C. Animals gravitated to her and she to them. Nana said that animals could sense the good in people. He wasn't sure that always applied, but in C.C.'s case, he believed it true. When the prince and his lackeys had spoken to C.C., he'd fought to keep from pummeling all of them into the ground. Men flirted constantly with Tatiana. It never bothered him.

He'd rationalized that the attention and suggestive comments were part of the high-profile life they both lived.

Michael had ignored the attention Tatiana received while she basked in it, drinking it in as though it were her life's blood. When the prince and his friends had flirted with C.C., however, he'd almost lost control. He'd wanted to shout, "Leave her alone. She belongs to me!"

The kitten scampered off into the garden, having apparently gotten its fill of human contact for the time being. C.C. leaned against Michael so naturally it felt as though they'd been a couple for years instead of hours. But they weren't a couple. Not really. All of this was make-believe. He had to keep reminding himself of that fact. Because if he didn't he would have to face his feelings for her.

Live in the moment.

It was one of Nana's sayings, and she had one for every occasion. She'd repeat this one when she thought he was being pulled down with memories and regret. Not for the first time, he realized her wisdom.

Live in the moment.

He put his arm around C.C.'s shoulders as she nestled into him. Most women would be hysterical, or angry, or both at what they'd gone through. She was calm. Under the circumstances she had every right to yell at him. Because of him she had been forced to flee the safety of the twenty-first century into the turbulent past, and now she had been forced again to flee the warmth and security of the tavern.

"This is all my fault," he said at last.

She reached up and touched his face with the back

of her hand. "This is not your fault."

Her touch warmed him to his core. "I should have changed kilts before we left the mansion."

"And I should have changed into more practical shoes."

"It's not the same."

She lifted an eyebrow. The gesture was so pixie-like, so cute, that it took all his will power not to gather her in his arms and kiss her.

"The reason I didn't change shoes," she began, "was because I wanted to prove to you that I could walk in heels like Tatiana."

He tucked a strand of hair behind her ear. He wanted to tell her he was glad she was not like Tatiana. But that he couldn't do. It might have opened the flood gates of his emotions. So he opted for another direction. "I wanted to show off that I had Scottish ancestry."

She smiled and laughed in a way that reminded him of wind chimes touched by a summer breeze. She pressed her hand against his chest. "See, we both were distracted."

He covered her hand with his. "That happens to me a lot whenever I'm around you."

"You were very gallant in the tavern, defending my honor."

His eyes narrowed. "That man was hitting on you."

"That man was Bonnie Prince Charlie. Historians say he flirts with everyone."

"I wouldn't care if he were the commissioner for the NFL. I didn't like how he was looking at you or talking to you."

She drew closer, resting both hands on his chest as she gazed into his eyes. "You're different. What happened to the Thinking Man statue?"

"Do you want him back?"

She shook her head slowly, giving him that slow smile that lit up her eyes like warm honey and cinnamon. "Absolutely not. I like this side of you. I'm just wondering." Her gaze slid toward the garden as a chuckle escaped. When she turned back, it looked as though she was struggling not to laugh. "It's like the episode in the original Star Trek TV series. I think it was the final season. The one where Mr. Spock travels back to the ice age and reverts to his inner caveman when he meets a woman." She paused. "You probably don't know what I'm talking about."

"You mean the episode named: 'All Our Yesterdays'? The woman's name was Zarabeth." He lifted his head and tried to keep his voice from giving away his amusement. "Actually, come to think of it, your theory makes a lot of sense. When we went through time I remember feeling different. As though my inner Neanderthal was being released."

She actually harrumphed at him and pinched his arm. "I don't believe you for a second."

"What gave me away?"

"You're grinning like a child who got away with eating an entire box of cookies."

Muffled shouts reached the alley and echoed to where they stood. The men from the tavern had circled back and were searching the side streets.

C.C. drew back into the shadows. "I think we'd have a better chance if we tried to blend into the crowd."

"Agreed, but not while I'm wearing the Campbell colors. I might as well be wearing a flashing beacon."

C.C. produced the fabric Fiona had given to her. "Fiona said this is a kilt, but it's in the old style, so it's one long piece. I can help you put it on, and…"

He held up his hand. "I can manage."

"But this is the old style of kilt," she pressed. "It's a length of wool that needs to be wrapped around your waist, slung over your shoulder, and belted in place."

"Again, I'll manage. I decided I wanted to embrace the whole Scottish kilt-wearing tradition."

C.C. scrunched her eyebrows together. "I still don't understand…" She sucked in her breath and her skin flushed. "Oh. You mean…"

He nodded. "Yup. Under this kilt I'm as naked as the day I was born."

Chapter Twenty-One

Church bells tolled the eight o'clock hour. The sound reverberated throughout the town, beckoning everyone to join in the celebration of Hogmanay. Young and old poured from their homes. The night was clear and crisp, a good omen to start the New Year, and for the moment C.C. felt safe. In the alley, she waited for Michael to arrange the yards of faded blue-and-black wool plaid Fiona had provided into a style that resembled a kilt.

They hadn't heard the men from the tavern for almost half an hour. She hoped they'd given up the chase. With her back to Michael, she averted her gaze and looked to her left, where the alleyway led to the town. On her right, the alley emptied into a park-like setting. From her vantage point, the clearing could be anything—land set aside for the town's use, complete with fairy trees, benches and flower beds, or the backyard of a rich merchant, or even a cemetery.

She heard Michael behind her, struggling with the volume of material. "Can I help?"

He mumbled, "No, thank you."

She allowed her gaze to drift toward the park again. A short while ago she'd joked that he was different. He'd joked back that he attributed it to their traveling back in time like Dr. Spock in a Star Trek episode. It was more than a change of place or time.

Some people thought that if they could change jobs, move to a different city, or date someone new, their lives would be better. The reality was more complicated. Her mother had often said that no matter where you went you were still the same person, with the same hopes and fears. Change had to come from within.

Michael thought this experience was changing him, but C.C. had seen the changes before they left the States.

He'd started changing when he was researching Scottish history for the movie part he wanted to play. He may not have realized it, but he had gone above and beyond what she suspected most people would have done. It was as though he'd become addicted to learning something new, or that he'd spent his life starving and had just discovered a pantry filled with all his favorite foods.

Michael swore under his breath, something about if he couldn't manage to belt the kilt in place, he'd walk out of the alley naked.

C.C. suppressed a giggle. "Are you sure you don't need my help?"

"If you promise not to laugh."

"I can't promise anything."

"Honesty. Fair enough."

She turned slowly, expecting...well, she wasn't sure what she expected. He had the wool fabric twisted loosely around his waist and draped over both shoulders. He held what looked like a death grip on the bunched fabric at his waist. "You seem to have the main idea," she said encouragingly. "And you're not naked."

"I will be if I let go. I can't get it to fit in place the right way."

She bit on her lip to keep from smiling. "How can I help?"

"If you can reach my belt..."

C.C. picked up the belt from the Campbell kilt on the ground. "You have the plaid too bunched up. You'll have to let go so I can readjust the fabric."

He lifted an eyebrow. "That wouldn't be a good idea."

"We'll go slowly, then." C.C. reached up to slip the wool down over his left shoulder. "If I can pull this through..." His breath was warm on her skin as she slipped it around and down. "You have too much material around your waist. We need to smooth out the folds."

Michael reached for her wrist. "I'll do it. Can you hold this section on my right side?"

She felt her face flush as she ducked her head, grateful for the long curls that hid her face from his view.

"Better," he said. "Now the belt. Once that's done, I'll take care of the sword and scabbard."

She handed it to him, and he secured it in place. "I'm the one who's done all this research, and yet you know how this type of kilt is worn. How is that possible?"

"Romance novels."

Chapter Twenty-Two

Cautiously, C.C. and Michael edged out of the alleyway toward the laughter and singing in the streets. Music seemed to chase away the frost in the air as the Scottish folk songs drew people into the streets. With the energy and crush of people, it no longer felt cold. The number of vendors and street performers had multiplied. Jugglers in bright colors entertained with knives, balls, and flaming batons. A section of the street was cordoned off for the dances now taking place.

Still holding her hand, Michael guided C.C. closer so they could view the dancing. Other observers like themselves made room for them. For one dance, couples faced each other, pacing the steps of what looked like a reel of some sort. Moving forward, they passed each other on the right, only to then dance backwards to their original place. The precision was amazing. Mesmerized, C.C. watched, trying to commit the steps to memory. In other dances, several couples took hands and formed circles, dancing around until they all became dizzy or dissolved into laughter and giggles.

The singing and laughter intensified with the tempo of the music. The notes of the fiddles lifted over the bagpipes as though the two instruments were in competition. People sang along with the melodies. The words to the songs became more raucous as the night marched toward the stroke of midnight.

There were silly songs:

"If all the world were paper and all the water ink.
If all the trees were bread and cheese.
What would I have to drink?"

And C.C. recognized a song from Shakespeare's Twelfth Night:

"When I was a bachelor, I led a merry life;
But now I am a married man and troubled with a wife."

But the song that brought the most reaction from the crowd was:

"John, come kiss me now, now, now;
And make no more ado."

The song was a clear signal to reach for your partner or to try and steal a kiss from a stranger. Couples gave in to the sport, laughed, and kissed. The musicians were aware of the magic they had created and slowed down their melodies. It would be at least a hundred or more years before slow dancing became fashionable, but couples found each other, breaking the rules. Others held hands or slipped into the shadows.

C.C. stood on the perimeter alongside Michael; it was as though they were observing a play. She glanced toward him, feeling shy for some reason. When he had challenged the advances of Bonnie Prince Charlie, it had been like an out-of-body experience for her, like she was a princess in a fairytale. Her girly side had almost thrown up her arms and cheered. Now she knew what a Super Bowl cheerleader felt like when she witnessed her team making the winning touchdown.

There had been a shift in their relationship without a word being spoken. It could be the romance of the place or the shared sense of danger that was the root of the change. She didn't care. Her mother had told her to live each moment as though tomorrow would never come. Those words had been tumbling through her mind all evening. When Michael had reached for her hand in the tavern, she hadn't hesitated. They had been thrown together into this adventure, and now they were a team. How long would it last?

Live in the moment.

Feeling bold, she squeezed his hand. As though he'd been as aware of her as she was of him, he immediately turned toward her. The expression in his eyes held a lifetime of questions.

She answered the one that was the easiest. "Yes, I'd love to dance with you."

Michael's eyes brightened with an inner light. He gave a slight nod and pulled C.C. into the street and into his arms. Instead of matching their steps to the tempo of the fiddle, he slowed them down even more so that the music flowed over and around them. He leaned toward her and pressed his head gently against hers. They were so close she could feel his heartbeat vibrate through her.

The world spun around her. The intimacy was intoxicating, and the music and laughter faded into the background. Absently, she noticed couples chasing each other in the streets, and laughing when they caught each other. A dog barked. Children played hide and seek. It was past their bedtime, she mused. She knew she was searching for distractions. Anything to keep from examining how she was feeling. It wasn't working.

Her emotions flew in dozens of directions at the

same time. They were dancing slowly, yet she was out of breath.

Michael pressed a kiss on the side of her head. "I've dreamed about holding you in my arms since the first time we met."

She trembled, not knowing how to react or what she wanted. That wasn't true. She knew exactly what she wanted. She wanted him to kiss her like he had at the wedding. She relived the moment. Had she known then? She knew she admired him and was frustrated that Tatiana took him for granted. C.C. had spent more than a few evenings alone wondering why he was interested in someone who couldn't make him smile. C.C. drew back to gaze at him. He was so close she could feel the warmth of his lips a half breath away.

"Nana told me to ask you out," he said, moving closer.

C.C. blinked, focusing on his eyes, his mouth. Did this man have any idea how wonderful he was? "Do you know why she might say that? I only spent a short time with her during Christmas dinner."

He nodded. "Her exact words were: 'If you don't ask that angel out, you're a fool.'"

"I'm no angel," she said, glancing away. She was crushing on a man who belonged to someone else.

"I never disagree with Nana. She's always right, especially when it comes to people."

He pulled her into his arms and her head rested against his chest. Her heart pounded so loud she was sure he could hear it beat. She had been nervous when he introduced her to his nana at Christmas. C.C. knew how important Michael's grandmother was to him, which created an irrational desire to make a good impression. And that was weird, she had chided herself. After all, she wasn't the girlfriend. She was the employee.

When she was introduced, his nana had immediately pulled C.C. into a warm embrace, asking about her family, her dreams, and finally what she thought about Michael.

She pulled away to look at him. "I just met your grandmother the one time," C.C. finally said.

"As I mentioned, she's a good judge of character. One meeting was all that she needed. That's when she asked me why I hadn't asked you out. I told her it was because I didn't know which answer I dreaded more from you: The one where you said yes, or the one where you said no."

He leaned toward her, and his lips parted. He was waiting for her answer. Her heart screamed to say yes. But he was Michael Campbell. What could he possibly see in her? And what about Tatiana?

She stood on her tiptoes to reach him. Her mouth brushed against his. Heat and promise in a touch. The music blended into the background, merging with the sights and sounds of the celebrations. A blend of blues, silvers, and greens. Second by second, the world drifted away. All that remained was Michael. She closed her eyes...

"We found him, lads," a man said, shattering the spell.

Michael was hit on the head from behind.

C.C. screamed as a man with a scar across his face grabbed her and yanked her away from Michael. He smelled of ale and sweat. She twisted in the man's arms and brought her heel down on the man's shoe. He yelped in pain and stumbled back, dropping his weapon. She scooped it up and rushed to Michael's side.

Michael had pulled his sword from its scabbard and now faced the bearded man from the tavern.

She struggled with the sword's weight and the effort to keep it level. It was heavier than it looked. "Don't come any closer," she shouted above the din of music and laughter. Her voice carried, silencing those in the immediate area.

The prince's men from the tavern, and more she didn't recognize, emerged from the crowd, weapons drawn.

Laughter erupted from the men who had attacked Michael. "I admire your grit," the bearded man said to C.C., "and we have your man surrounded. Ye can barely hold the blade. I can see it in your gaze. Ye have neither the stomach nor the strength to use such a man's weapon. We are not here for you, lass. We are here for your man."

Fiona stepped out from the crowd, with Liam beside her. Both held swords. "We're here to even the odds. I'll thank you to leave our friends alone."

"Stand aside," the bearded man said.

"And let you harm them? I most certainly will not." She leveled her sword at the man's throat. "Ye all know me and that I never stand aside. You're a drunk and a bully. There's nothing for ye here."

The bearded man hesitated. "We all saw it in the Water Horse tavern. This man wore the Campbell colors. The clan is known to harbor sympathy to England, and thus he is an enemy to Bonnie Prince Charlie and our cause. I have my orders."

"Wearing the Campbell colors was an innocent mistake," Fiona said. "As you can see, he discarded them. His accent clearly signals that he is from the American colonies. The Americans are not your enemy. They too, struggle under England's rule."

The man with the scar, who had grabbed C.C., whispered to the bearded man. Their heated exchange resulted in nods of agreement and the bearded man sheathing his weapon. "Very well," he said. "But this is not over."

Liam kept his sword ready until the men dispersed, then said to Fiona, "That was odd."

"Everyone's on edge, that's all."

"We'd better get C.C. and Michael away from the celebrations."

Fiona nodded and sheathed her sword as she turned toward the two time-travelers. "I know a few of these men. They are looking for a fight. There is a vacant cottage a short distance from here, along the shoreline. It has a blue door, an herb garden, and a lit candle in the window. You will be safe there until it's time for you to return. When the church bells chime eleven o'clock, you can head for your rendezvous with William and the coach. Until then, you need to stay as far away from the town as possible. Just make sure you reach the rendezvous location on time."

Chapter Twenty-Three

They'd been walking for what seemed like over an hour, but C.C. knew that couldn't be true as she heard church bells calling out the time. She pulled her cloak around her against the frosted breeze. Snowflakes swirled in the air, prelude to a storm.

Finding the cottage Fiona had mentioned was more difficult than she had suggested. All the cottages along the shore so far had either a blue door without a candle in the window, or a candle without the blue door. One of the things they all had in common, however, was an herb garden.

But it was so romantic. Even though it was the dead of winter in Inverness, Scotland, C.C. felt as though she could go on walking with Michael like this forever. The crescent moon and the stars had come out from behind the clouds. In the distance, light from the various bonfires combined to help guide them. A few rowboats were tied to pilings, indicating that the water was deep even close to shore.

Michael slowed. "There's a cottage that looks like the one Fiona described," he said, breaking into her thoughts. "I'll make sure it's safe. I'll just be a few minutes."

C.C. concentrated on her footing. By now, it was likely the bearded man and his friends had spread the word that a member of the Campbell clan was in

111

Inverness. She was grateful Fiona had wanted them to leave.

She shivered, pulled her cloak around her even tighter, and blew on her hands. Michael had told her to stay put. "Where does he think I'm going to go?" she muttered under her breath. This was nuts. She couldn't stand still. She had to keep moving or she'd freeze to death. Okay, maybe not freeze to death. That was a little over the top, but she was very cold. She should have asked Fiona for a pair of boots. The Cinderella slippers looked breathtakingly beautiful, but they pinched her feet and were useless against the cold.

Making sure she kept in sight the location where Michael had gone, she traced a path back and forth along the shoreline. A small shadow darted past her. It looked like the same snow-white kitten she'd seen in the alley. Had it followed her? More likely, it was one of many kittens with the same coloring in Inverness.

It padded along the lip of the frozen shoreline, alternating between sniffing the tall grasses and taking a delicate bite. It gave a series of soft meows as though chatting with C.C., then suddenly let out a high-pitched scream and splashed into the water.

The kitten had fallen in.

C.C. rushed as close as she dared to the edge of the shore. Under the glow of the moon, a circle of ripples spread out from where she'd seen the kitten disappear. She called out to it, as though that would help. Seconds ticked by until it surfaced a short distance away. She sighed with relief just as a new fear set in. Cats didn't like the water. Did they even know how to swim? The current pulled the kitten toward the center of the river as the little animal thrashed around and cried out.

Easing still closer to the water, C.C. tried to reach it by extending her arm, but the current and the animal's efforts to keep his head above water only succeeded in moving the animal farther away. C.C. inched her way forward until she stood in the half-submerged marshy grasses.

She sucked in her breath as ice-cold water lashed against her skin. Keeping pace with the progress of the kitten as it drifted along, C.C. sloshed through the grasses and once again reached out. She was still too far away.

C.C. took another step closer to the kitten and lost her footing. She screamed and plunged into the river. Ice-cold needles shot through her. She forced down the panic and fought back to the surface, gasping for breath.

Her legs tangled in both the long material of her dress and the thick underwater plants. Disoriented, like the time she'd bodysurfed and been caught in an undertow, she tried to tamp down her growing panic. All she could see was water.

C.C. splashed in the same way the kitten had moments before, and with the same results. She was being pulled closer and closer to the center of the river. Even if Michael realized she'd fallen in, would he be able to find her in time?

Something brushed against her legs. She screamed as thoughts of crocodiles and water snakes entered her thoughts. Breathing heavily, she tried to calm down.

Great. Just great. She was drowning, and irrational thoughts of being torn to bits by imaginary monsters were not helpful.

She pushed the thoughts from her mind, willing

herself to concentrate on keeping her head above water. Her body went numb. She couldn't feel her legs. She didn't know how much longer she could keep her head above water. How long before hypothermia set in? Minutes? Seconds?

****

Michael dove into the icy currents of the River Ness and surfaced a short distance from C.C. He'd heard her scream but hadn't been able to reach her in time. She had been pulled into the center of the river. Miraculously, her head was still above the surface, but she was losing her fight. Her eyes were half closed and her arms limp as she began to sink beneath the dark waters.

He intensified his efforts to reach her, and in a few clean strokes he was close enough to pull her head above water. Her body sagged against him like a rag doll, and she gasped for breath. Her eyes fluttered shut.

He shook her gently. "Stay awake," he ordered, knowing there was panic in his voice. He fought against the numbing cold and his mounting fear as he swam toward shore. She was breathing and conscious. That was something. He held onto that ray of hope.

Once he was on solid ground, he raced toward the vacant cottage he'd found earlier. When he kicked open the door, he found the wood fire he'd built to surprise her had already warmed the one room of the cottage. He put her down in front of the hearth and rubbed her arms and legs. She was shaking, and her lips had turned blue with the cold, but she was awake.

"We have to get you out of these clothes."

She nodded slowly. Her voice was so faint he had to lean forward to hear. "The fire's nice. Who made it?"

He started to answer her question, but she slumped against him, unconscious.

Chapter Twenty-Four

A log in the fireplace shifted, sending amber sparks into the chimney and warm heat throughout the cottage. Candles burned on a table near a window, and a cupboard displaying china plates painted with blue and yellow wildflowers hung on the far wall next to a rocking chair. C.C. leaned against Michael's chest. She'd never felt so content. She snuggled in Michael's embrace under the layers of blankets. She flexed her fingers. Her hands and feet still tingled from exposure to the cold water, but she knew she was out of danger.

She didn't know how long it had been since he'd rescued her; she'd drifted in and out of consciousness only to have Michael call her back each time. She did remember that he'd turned away when she took off her clothes and bundled up in the blanket. Her clothes were draped over a chair to dry, but she had lost her wedding slippers when her legs and feet tangled in the underwater grasses.

The snow-white kitten that had caused all the trouble lay curled beside the hearth. The ball of fluff opened its eyes and gave C.C. a typical catlike blank stare. C.C. liked to think that the kitten was saying thank you and gave it a nod. The kitten closed its eyes once more and purred.

The steady rise and fall of Michael's breathing was comforting, and the small cottage felt like an enchanted place where time really could stand still.

"How are you feeling?" he said. His voice was deep and rich and seemed to add warmth to the air.

She loved the sound of his voice. It made her feel... No, don't go down that path. She kept her focus on the dancing flames and the sleeping kitten. "I feel well," she said, knowing that wasn't even close to what she was feeling. "Thank you for saving me."

"You are welcome." He pulled her closer against his chest. "What were you doing so close to the shoreline?"

She nodded to the kitten, which had opened its eyes again to stare in their direction as though it knew it was the topic of conversation. "I was trying to save that little beastie."

The kitten let out a protesting meow, rose, stretched, and then padded over to C.C. and licked her toes. Its pink tongue was wet and as rough as fine sandpaper against her skin.

"That tickles." Laughing, C.C. pulled her feet under the blankets before she bent to scratch behind the kitten's ear as it settled beside her. "You're forgiven, little one."

"You have a forgiving heart, Cinderella Charming."

She liked that he'd used her full name. She knew her parents had named her after the folktale character out of love. She'd forgotten that until recently. C.C. shifted under the blanket. "I don't deserve your praise, I'm afraid. I haven't always been so forgiving. It's just that lately I'm remembering my mother's sayings. I think that's because it's quieter in this time period. My mother had one for every occasion, like, 'Many hands make light work,' when she wanted all of us to help with gardening or housework, or, 'A watched pot never boils,' when we kept asking when dinner would be ready."

"Do you have a favorite?"

"I'm not sure if it's one of my favorites, but it's the one that I can't stop thinking about. If we were fighting amongst ourselves, as siblings sometimes do, or complaining about one of our school friends, she'd say, 'It's more important to let go than to hold onto the past.' "

"I like that." He leaned his head against hers. The gesture felt so normal and so right. The cottage was snug and warm, and with Michael's arms wrapped around her, she couldn't imagine anywhere else she'd rather be. But Michael was used to living large, especially when he traveled. He'd stayed in penthouses, suites, and places that came with their own butler and cook.

"This place must seem so small and cramped to you," she said, breaking the comfortable silence.

She felt him take a deep breath as he adjusted the blanket around her shoulders, encasing them both in its warmth. "I grew up in a place not much larger than this one," he said. "I haven't thought about Nana's home in a long time. She used to like sayings, as well, and the ones you've mentioned are a lot like some of the ones my grandmother says. However, one of her favorites is one that's been in my mind a lot lately: 'Dreams become real when you share them with someone you love.' "

"That's beautiful." She turned her head to the side, trying to see his face, but it was lost in the shadows.

"Your bio said you grew up in a wealthy neighborhood in California, were home-schooled by private tutors, and when your parents died, you inherited a fortune."

"The home-schooling part was true. Nana felt the only way to keep me away from the gangs in our neighborhood was to teach me herself."

C.C. turned in his arms. "But your bio said..."

He scrunched his eyebrows together. "There's a lot in my bio that's not true. But could you turn around again? You're not wearing anything under the blankets. The tabloids may claim I'm made of stone, but..." He chuckled. "Another urban myth, by the way." A mischievous smile played along the corners of his mouth. "I'm very human, and you're a beautiful woman. It's hard not to stare."

She was mesmerized by his smile, his compliment—and then his words registered. She glanced down. The corner of the blanket had slipped dangerously low. Her face felt like it had burst into flame. She snapped the blankets higher and spun around to face the fireplace, remembering the female fans who threw themselves at him on a daily basis. Most of them were dressed in tight clothes that left little to the imagination. She didn't want him to think she was like that. "I'm so sorry. I didn't mean..."

The kitten, as though feeling C.C.'s unease, nuzzled against her leg for attention. C.C. bent down and gathered it onto her lap, processing what he'd said. She felt as though she were in a dream, where there were such things as princesses and handsome princes.

He chuckled again and sat up a little straighter. "New topic. I know you come from a big family. What was that like? I'm an only child."

C.C. petted the kitten behind its ears, still processing what he'd said about her being beautiful. No one had called her that in her whole life. Cute, perhaps, when she was a child, but certainly not beautiful.

She kissed the kitten on the top of its head, hoping her cheeks didn't look as flushed as they felt. "My family was middle class. My dad was an engineer for Boeing, and my mom worked as a school secretary in the high school we all attended. They were doting parents, went to all our events, from sports to spelling bee competitions to science fairs. They displayed our ribbons and trophies proudly around the house and always said we could be anything we wanted to be. I know some people like to criticize that type of parenting and say those parents are raising children who will fail because they don't understand that the world is a harsh, unforgiving place. I disagree. We knew we were loved. I may have floundered in college, trying to find the right major, but I was grateful they never judged me. Knowing there was someone on my side who loved me, no matter what, made it feel like I really could succeed." Her voice trailed off. "But then it all fell apart."

He wrapped his arms around her a little tighter. "Do you mind me asking what happened?"

C.C. felt her breath catch. "My...my mother died just after my second year in college, and our father remarried four months later. That marriage didn't last long." She concentrated on breathing. Michael's touch and reliving her past regrets were jumbled together. "To this day I've never asked what happened between my father and my stepmother. If I'm honest, I was glad when they broke up, which made me feel worse."

He reached around to pet the kitten now sleeping on her lap. "I'm a self-proclaimed expert on the feeding and care of guilt. My experience is that it never gives you peace, only more pain. Is guilt over your father's failed marriage the reason you don't visit your family? You're still mad at your dad?"

His hands looked enormous as he petted the kitten gently. He was a mixture of strength and tenderness. A warrior on the football field and yet interested in her family issues. Did Tatiana know how wonderful he was?

She leaned her head against his chest. "I know it sounds childish. I'm still trying to forgive my father, or forgive myself for waiting so long to forgive him." She sighed. "My explanation sounds like a crazed merry-go-round." She hesitated, then continued to answer his question with, "Yes, I'm still mad at him, and now he's sick."

The kitten sat up, yawned, stretched, and leapt down from C.C.'s lap and headed over to the hearth, where it walked around in a circle before curling down for another nap.

C.C. stared at it until the image blurred. "Can we change the subject? I seem to be saying that a lot lately." But when he nodded, she asked, "Why was I chosen to be your bride? I didn't think Tatiana's mother liked me, and she makes all the decisions."

"Alba doesn't like most people, but I had the sense that she didn't have many options, and she was in a hurry for some reason. I think Alba is more interested in Tatiana getting a speedy divorce than Tatiana is. Plus, she doesn't consider you a threat and liked that you had zero knowledge about football. She felt it supported the story that we had nothing in common."

He'd grown serious. The kitten had opened its eyes as though it too sensed the change. She decided that would never do. "I take notes at our meetings," she blurted. "And I purchased the book *Football for Dummies*."

He kissed her shoulder. "Yes, you did. You have a notebook full of notes, as I remember. And as for that book, I'm not sure it's the best source. After you finished reading it, you said the game was boring."

The warm touch of his lips on her skin lingered. The kitten had closed its eyes, and the fire burned brighter. She laughed softly. "No, what I said was that *you* were boring. When you have the football, you either complete the pass or run it in for a touchdown. The opposing team doesn't have a chance."

He chuckled. "We should give the losing team a trophy when we win. Then they wouldn't feel so bad."

She elbowed him in the ribs and turned to gaze at him. "I know you're joking, but you should see the losing team's faces. They look so sad."

He touched the side of her face with his fingers. "Nana was right. You have a kind heart."

"You were getting too serious, and I wanted to lighten the mood."

He brushed a strand of hair behind her ear. "Nana also says I'm too serious. A lifetime spent running from my past is to blame, I suspect."

She turned to face him, making sure the blanket was secure. "You don't have to tell me, but you said there were discrepancies in your bio. Did the reporters find out? Is that the real reason we had to leave?"

"It feels foolish now. Our past can define us. My

father was a minor league football player. A defensive lineman. He didn't know when to stop hitting people. He was always getting into fistfights and ending up in the hospital. That's where my parents met. My mother was a nurse, and she was on call one night when he was brought in to the hospital. I'm not sure how long they were together, but when he found out she was pregnant, he took off. He died in a bar fight before I was born. My mother moved in with Nana but died before I learned to walk. Nana moved us to the West Coast and changed our names. My grandmother didn't want me to be defined by who my father was and the things he'd done."

C.C. reached up and kissed him lightly on the lips. "You are not your father."

"Nana always says the same thing." He cupped her face in his hands, his eyes searching hers. "Do you know the reason Tatiana's mother doesn't like you?"

She shook her head, hypnotized by the warmth in his eyes.

"She accused me of being attracted to you. Tatiana laughed it off as ridiculous, said you weren't my type, and recited Alba's belief that we have nothing in common. Did you know that your eyes are the color of gold in the firelight?"

C.C. held her breath. They were alone in a romantic setting and literally many lifetimes away from the twenty-first century and their reality. It would be so easy to close her eyes and pretend that tomorrow would never come. This was one of the flaws in living life in the moment. There had to be boundaries. She didn't want a one-night stand, and she sensed neither did Michael. She wanted a forever after.

He was engaged to Tatiana. It was one thing to kiss at the altar as part of a script. This would be something else. She drew back, and felt him do the same. "I think I heard the church bells."

His expression turned into an emotionless mask, as though he'd also realized they'd stepped too close to the edge. "We should head to the rendezvous point." He cleared his throat and moved farther away. "William will be waiting. Your clothes are dry, and Fiona left a pair of boots here for you to wear. I'll go outside and give you a chance to dress." Michael disentangled from the blanket and left the cottage without another word.

She sat huddled in the blanket and looked over at the kitten. "What a mess."

When Michael left, it felt as though he'd taken all the warmth in the cottage with him. Why couldn't he be one of those guys that when you got to know them you realized they were terrible people?

One consolation was that she'd achieved her goal of making him laugh. Well, if not a full-out laugh, a chuckle, at least. Yes, clearly a chuckle. The man never cracked a smile, and yet not only was he behaving more like a human being, he had shared part of his life, a part he'd kept hidden from the world. She understood now why his nana was so protective of him and he so devoted to her. The sadness reflected in his eyes when he spoke about his parents had made her want to take him in her arms and kiss away the pain.

"Stop daydreaming," she said aloud. "He's marrying Tatiana. Your marriage to Michael is a fake."

The startled kitten woke and let out a protesting meow.

C.C. gave an apologetic shrug and reached for her

clothes. She slipped the gown over her head, wondering why the mental image of Michael in Tatiana's arms made her want to throw things. But as upset as she was, she couldn't stay mad at Tatiana. She was as much a pawn as C.C. This was all Alba's doing. She'd placed C.C. and Michael together.

The kitten meowed again, padding over to curl around C.C.'s legs.

C.C. bent down and scratched the kitten under its chin. "I couldn't agree more. If for some reason Alba travels back to this time, you have my permission to cough up a really big furball in her most expensive shoes."

Chapter Twenty-Five

Michael and C.C. neared the rendezvous in silence. Michael cast a quick glance over at C.C. She'd been unusually quiet, and it didn't take a genius to understand the reason. A short time ago Fiona had joined them, along with Liam, and the two of them had said very little, as well.

There was a weight in the air that had nothing to do with the impending storm. Shadows spilled over the pathways and highlighted fallen trees. The quiet beauty quivered in the moon's glow as though waiting for a noise to break the spell. It struck Michael that he wasn't ready to return to his own time.

In this century, no one knew that he was a big-deal football player. The type of coffee he drank or the books he read wouldn't make national news. True, he'd been chased and attacked. He took the blame for that. Wearing the Campbell plaid at this time and place in history was a boneheaded move.

He wasn't looking forward to getting back to reality, despite the possible movie deal. He had been offered other movie roles before the one for *Highland Rebel*, everything from lone-wolf detectives to super heroes to an international spy. The only one that had interested him had been the retelling of the real life story of the Scottish hero Rob Roy.

But even that prospect had lost its shine. It was

more than dealing with the press. His feelings for C.C. had deepened. He couldn't imagine his life without her.

The snap of a twig under Michael's boots sent birds retreating into the dark sky from the tree branches where they'd been resting. He flinched, looking toward the sky.

C.C. reached over and touched his arm. "Is everything okay?"

He wanted to pull her into his arms. Ask her to stay here with him. He couldn't. Correction. He wouldn't. Instead, he nodded and watched her move away to join Fiona and Liam in the clearing.

It was almost midnight. The air crackled with tension, reflecting his mood. He was in real danger, but danger of his own making. He didn't blame C.C. for being frustrated with him at the cottage. He'd mishandled everything. He had been about to kiss her.

He knew it.

She knew it.

Even the kitten knew it.

He'd also sensed that there was a real possibility that their kiss would have led to their making love. But what would happen the next day? He knew she'd come to the same conclusion. He'd allowed his feelings for her to go too far.

He pushed the self-recriminations down and settled on the present. Focusing on the present had always served him well. He got into trouble when he dwelt too long on the past or on the future.

He stepped out of the forest into the clearing to join C.C., Liam, and Fiona under a ceiling of stars. Michael had expected to see the coach. "Shouldn't William be here by now? Are you sure we have the right place?"

Fiona rested her hand on the hilt of her blade. "William will be here."

"Except he's never late," Liam said.

Fiona's voice was even. "William will be here," she repeated. "He knows the consequences if we don't make it back in time."

"Couldn't we take a boat to Urquhart Castle?" C.C. offered.

Liam unsheathed his sword. "Did you hear something?" He turned around slowly, peering into the shadows. "I swear I saw a flash of steel. Probably my imagination." He turned to C.C. "You suggested a boat. It's out of the question. Even if the Loch Ness Monster weren't a factor, traveling by water would take too long. We'd never make it by midnight."

"Out of curiosity," Michael said, "just what would happen if we didn't make it back by midnight?"

Liam and Fiona exchanged shadowed expressions Michael couldn't decipher. "You don't have to worry," Fiona said. "William will make it here in time."

C.C.'s mouth curved in a nervous smile. "See, Michael, we have nothing to worry about. Liam, you mentioned the Loch Ness Monster. That suggests that you believe Nessie is real. I know this sounds crazy, but when I fell into the river, it felt as though something kept me afloat until Michael reached me."

"Oh, aye," Liam said. "I believe in everything. That is what keeps me alive."

The two of them continued to discuss sightings of Nessie throughout history. Normally, Michael would have been intrigued. Not this time. Two points stood out for him. The first was that as improbable as it seemed, something *had* helped keep C.C. safe until he could rescue her. He vowed never to make fun of the belief in Nessie again. And the second was that he knew by the tone of C.C.'s laughter that she was as on edge as the rest of them. She was using stories of Nessie to distract everyone from dwelling too long on what could be keeping William.

****

"Can we talk?"

Michael recognized the tone in C.C.'s voice and the significance of those three words. Never in the history of relationships did what happened after they were spoken turn out well.

He nodded, bracing himself.

She blew on her hands. "Waiting for William to arrive is making me more nervous." She motioned for him to follow her a short distance from Fiona and Liam.

The dappled glow of moonlight filtered through a canopy of trees as C.C. turned toward him, hands on hips. "We should discuss what will happen when we return."

"What if William doesn't make it here before midnight?"

"Fiona isn't worried."

Michael lifted an eyebrow.

C.C. waved away his concern. "I can't think about that now. I need to talk about us."

Michael could only nod. He felt the tension rising between them. For a short while they'd been in a protective cocoon, and now it was coming to an end. He wanted to shout out that he wished it could be different between them, but reality kept him quiet and rooted him to the ground.

He would not, could not, abandon Tatiana.

Abandonment was something his father had done. "I no longer care about the reporters, if that's why you're concerned. I'll tell them anything they want to know. Let the chips fall where they may, as the saying goes." He knew that wasn't what she meant, but saying it aloud made it real. C.C.'s kind, non-judgmental nature had helped him face his fears as well as his past.

"Good for you." Her voice was whisper-thin. She placed her hand on the trunk of an oak tree as though to draw strength from its core. "I know we rehearsed what we were going to say. It's just..." She shook her head. "You were right from the beginning. This was a bad idea. I had a crush on you, and that's when I didn't know you very well. Now...well..." She moved to lean against the tree. "I'm sorry we kissed, and I'm sorry we spent time here together."

"I'm not."

"How can you say that? You're engaged to Tatiana. This whole setup was designed not only to repair your reputation but to take the attention off the two of you long enough so that Tatiana could get a divorce and the two of you could marry."

Michael wanted to reach out to her. Pull her into his arms. Instead he stood as still as the oak tree. She was right. All of it. He'd given in to his feelings for her. When he was with C.C. he was happy, happier than he'd ever thought possible. She made him smile, but he was engaged to Tatiana. More than that. Tatiana was pregnant with his child. He'd made a promise to her, and he wouldn't go back on his word. Breaking promises was something his father had done. His father had not cared who he hurt as long as it got him what he wanted. Michael wouldn't do that to C.C. or to Tatiana.

"I'm sorry," he said, knowing the words weren't enough.

She looked away. "No, I'm the one who's sorry. I knew what I was doing. My eyes were wide open. We faked our marriage, but I can't fake how I feel about you. Everyone will know the moment they see us together. I want to leave Scotland as soon as possible. Can you deal with the reporters by yourself?"

He gave her a quick nod and cleared his throat. He wasn't as good as she thought about hiding his emotions. That was probably the reason Tatiana's mother had been against the fake marriage later in the day, even though she had started the whole idea. She had seen exactly how Michael felt about C.C. whether or not he had known it himself.

C.C. brushed past him and headed toward the clearing. "We should get back to Fiona and Liam," she said over her shoulder.

"There's something you should know first," he said. "We really are married."

She turned abruptly, her eyes wide. "To each other?" She let out a breath. "That was a stupid comment," she said through clenched teeth. "Of course you meant to each other. You wouldn't have said it if it weren't true. I'm assuming Father O'Malley is a real priest."

"Yes."

"And the mountain of paperwork I signed?"

"One of the documents was a marriage license."

Her gaze flitted from Michael, down to the ground, and then back again. Her breath labored, she crossed her arms over her chest. Her hands were clenched so tightly the knuckles shone white in the moonlight.

"Setting aside the whole issue that you tricked me, I'm assuming Tatiana knew this part as well?"

Michael rubbed the back of his neck. "She and her mother didn't want to take any chances that Tatiana's husband would discover our marriage wasn't real. Harold thought it too risky to hire an actor to play the part of a priest. He was sure the man might leak it to the press before the ceremony. It was Lady Roselyn's suggestion that we ask Father O'Malley."

"Tatiana put on a good performance," C.C. said under her breath. She walked a few steps toward the clearing and then marched back to face him. Her jaw was set. "Because this is a real marriage, we'll have to file for an annulment or a divorce. Annulment would be simplest."

Michael noted that C.C. sounded deceptively calm. He was getting to know her and understood that at the moment she had her emotions on a tight leash. That was for the best. All they had to do was get through the next few hours, and it would all be over. "Tatiana doesn't want you and me to get an annulment. She wants the drama and media attention of a divorce. She doesn't want her husband to suspect it was all staged."

"What do you want?"

"I'm not sure," he lied.

"Divorce it is." She gave him a thin smile. There was pain behind the smile that tore at his heart. "Did I mention to you that my brother is a divorce attorney?" C.C said. "A really good one. When he finds out that I'm filing for a divorce from the famous quarterback Michael Campbell, he will want…" She shook her head. "My brother will *demand* that he be allowed to examine the divorce papers before I sign. In less time than it takes for you to throw a football pass, my brother will realize that I never signed a prenuptial agreement."

Michael did the only thing he could. He nodded. "I get your point."

"I don't think you do." She balled up her fists. "You kissed me like it meant something. I thought... I don't know what I thought. Then you spring it on me that we're really married. And while I'm processing that revelation, thinking that it might be a sign we should stay together, you calmly discuss whether we should get an annulment or a divorce. I'm an idiot. I was swept up in the romance of our *adventure*, as the sisters like to call whatever this is. Nothing that happened between us was real." Her voice rose and caught as she took a breath. She crossed her arms over her chest again as though she needed them there to keep from falling apart. "Nothing meant anything to you, other than a way to pass the time. I'm not like you. I'm flesh and blood. I'm not made of stone. I can't turn my emotions on and off." She pressed her lips together. "On second thought, when I talk to my brother I'm going to ask him to see if he can take you for everything the law allows."

He kept his voice disciplined, even. He wouldn't allow himself to think too much right now. "I'll let Harold know not to contest anything."

Her voice broke. "Why are you doing this...really?"

"I told you."

C.C. placed her hand on Michael's arm. Her voice softened as she blinked away tears. "Something else is going on with you. I can feel it. I know you don't love

Tatiana. I'm not blind. I'm not asking you to choose between us: I just want the truth. I'm asking as a friend. Please."

He looked away. "Tatiana is pregnant."

Chapter Twenty-Six

Michael's announcement echoed in C.C.'s mind. He hadn't said a word more. She knew he was watching her, waiting for a reaction. Surprisingly, she felt at peace.

Tatiana was pregnant.

C.C. should have suspected that was the real reason Tatiana was in a rush to get a divorce after months of delays. Tatiana and Michael hadn't been behaving like a couple in love for some time. It wasn't that they were fighting. It was the indifference.

Michael stood waiting for her to judge him. How could she? He was doing the right thing. If anything, she loved him more.

She stood on tiptoes, smiled warmly, and kissed him on the cheek. It was her way of saying good-bye.

The clearing erupted as William's coach thundered into view. Startled, C.C. turned toward the commotion. William struggled to control the horses, shouting to Fiona and Liam as he reined in the team. Fiona and Liam grabbed onto the lead horse as William continued to shout for them to hurry, adding, "I think I was followed."

C.C. and Michael raced to the clearing. Out of breath, C.C. approached the coach. She remembered her impression of it when they'd first traveled back in time. It was not exactly as she'd imagined a Cinderella coach would look, but it was close—copper and wood polished to a high gloss, painted images of braided vines and wildflowers outlining doors and windows, and white horses, bright as new snow.

She knew the coach before her was the same one by its markings, but it looked like it had driven through a storm of mud. Only glimpses of the painted vines and flowers were visible through the dirt and grime. The horses had suffered the same fate as the coach. Their sides heaved as they sucked in breath through flared nostrils.

William yanked his rifle from the bench's boot and jumped down from the coach. His clothes were as disheveled and transformed as the coach and horses. "I think I was followed," he repeated.

Fiona stroked the lead horse's nose while Liam asked Michael to help him rub down the other horses. "The woods are full of shadows and sounds this time of year," Fiona said. "We've never had any trouble before." She paused. "Where did you get that gun? It looks like it belongs in a museum. Is the rifle from the right century?"

William smoothed his hand over the barrel. "It's always been with the coach. This is the first time I've felt the need to make sure it was loaded."

C.C. stepped forward. "To answer Fiona's question, I believe it is eighteenth century. I know a little about guns. This type of weapon was used in the battle of Culloden by both British and Scottish troops. It has a faster reload time than its predecessors, but it also has a powerful kick when fired."

When both Fiona and William gaped at her, she shrugged. "Michael's not the only one who knows history trivia."

"We should get going," Liam said, coming over to Fiona. "The horses are strong, but I don't want them standing in the cold any longer than necessary. They need to keep moving. So do we. The clock doesn't stop its countdown just because we take a break."

Fiona rolled her eyes. "You may play the part of a juggler, but you do not have a sense of humor."

The crack of a rifle tore through the forest. Liam dove in front of Fiona. The force of the bullet pushed his shoulder back against Fiona as they both hit the ground.

The lead horse reared. William fought to bring it under control as Michael pulled C.C. to the ground and covered her with his body. William fired into the woods.

Another shot.

The bullet lodged in the side of the coach. The horses whinnied and pawed the ground.

"We're outnumbered," William shouted, reaching for his powder to reload. "One rifle against many."

C.C. sprang to her feet and reached for William's rifle. "You drive. I'm a good shot."

"She's right," Michael said. "The horses are ready to bolt. We need to get out of here."

William nodded and climbed back into the driver's seat. C.C. leveled the rifle in the direction she'd last heard a shot, while Michael helped Fiona get Liam into the coach and waited for C.C.

She squeezed the trigger. The recoil of the rifle pushed her back as William snapped the reins over the horse's rumps. The coach lurched forward.

Michael scooped C.C. into his arms and dived into

the moving coach as another round of bullets sprayed the clearing.

****

C.C. braced against the side of the coach. The forest sped past as the horses raced toward Urquhart Castle. The danger had become real. She gulped in air like she'd finished a marathon She had kept the rifle with her, reloaded and ready. It was one thing to shoot a gun at a target or into the forest. But could she aim a gun at a person and pull the trigger? She shivered. She honestly didn't know.

"Do you know who attacked us?" C.C. rubbed her shoulder where the butt of the rifle had bruised her.

Bending over to tend Liam's wound, Fiona gave a slight shake of her head.

"Where'd you learn how to shoot?" Michael asked.

C.C. knew Fiona was avoiding her question, and Michael was using C.C.'s tactic of changing the topic. Normally, she'd be frustrated at the change in subject, but the alternative was a full scale freakout.

She sat up a little straighter. "Remember I said my family was into fairytales?" When he nodded, she continued. "What better place to wear our costumes than at a medieval faire? My parents thought while we were there we should take advantage of all the classes being offered. In addition to the candle, pottery, and soap-making classes..." She paused to look over at Michael and mimicked the kind of face she might make if she bit into a sour lemon. "I was a total failure at all three of those. Thankfully, there were also ones that taught weaponry. You saw that I'm not very good with a sword. They're just too heavy, and I kept cutting my fingers on the edges. It became obvious that I was more likely to injure myself than someone else." She grinned. "I discovered, however, that I am very good with a gun."

Fiona tore material from the hem of her skirt and pressed the wadded material against Liam's wound. "You and Michael were a big help. Thank you." She exchanged a glance with Liam. "Do you think Bonnie Prince Charlie and his men attacked us? It's common knowledge that they don't like the Campbells, and Michael wearing their clan tartan made him a target earlier."

"Anything is possible," Liam said, wincing. "I think you're making my wound worse. Are you sure you know what you're doing?"

"I was a field nurse. I know what I'm doing. If it was the prince's men, it doesn't make any sense that they would take the trouble to attack us."

"Agreed. Why waste the ammunition? It's common knowledge that their stores are depleted. The prince gave strict orders to conserve their reserves in anticipation of their battle with the English in the spring."

The coach rolled over something on the road and threw Fiona off balance. Michael helped her back up. She nodded a thank you and regained her position beside Liam before she tore off another strip of cloth and pressed it to his shoulder. "I agree," Fiona said. "I don't understand why they would risk wasting their ammunition, either." She frowned at Liam. "You weren't supposed to get hurt. No one was."

"Yeah, well, we all knew the risks."

C.C. noticed that Fiona's words sounded deceptively calm. A muscle along her jawline flexed as she pressed her lips together before she said, "Except, we hired you because you said you were the best. That you were an expert with any weapon made by man or beast, and that you could keep everyone safe."

"And here I thought it was because you thought I was cute."

Her lips trembled as she kept pressure on his wound and looked as though she struggled with either bursting into tears or throwing Liam out of the coach. "Your brother is cute. You are annoying."

He reached for her hand. "Then why did you agree to our betrothal?"

She moved away. "Neither one of us had a choice, remember? Stop changing the subject. You weren't supposed to get shot."

"I'm not bulletproof." He winced. "Hey, are you deliberately pressing too hard?"

She shrugged. "Maybe." She narrowed her gaze. "You leapt in front of me."

"I was trying to save you."

Fiona's hand trembled as she tied the bandage in place. "I can take care of myself." She paused. "You could have been killed. Then where would we be?"

"I'm expendable. You aren't. There have to be three matchmakers or the enchantment won't work." He leaned against the back wall of the coach and shut his eyes. "On second thought, next time I'll let them shoot you."

Michael leaned toward C.C. and whispered, "Do you know what is going on between them?"

"Fiona said they don't like each other. Paraphrasing Shakespeare, 'I fear they do protest too much.' "

Chapter Twenty-Seven

Most of the ride to Urquhart Castle had been in silence. Fiona and Liam had continued to bicker, but there was something about how Liam's gaze lingered on Fiona when she looked away that told a different story. There was a time C.C. had hoped that was how Michael looked at her. Even if it were true, C.C. pledged she would no longer dwell on the possibilities of being together with Michael. Tatiana and Michael were going to have a baby, and his focus needed to be on his family.

C.C.'s eyes brimmed with tears as she forced herself to gaze out the coach window. The dark forest sped past in a blur. She wanted the last few hours she'd spent with Michael to be a dream. She wanted to wake up, knowing that everything was back to the way it had been before she'd traveled back in time. When they were only friends. Before she agreed to a fake marriage, before she realized how much she loved him.

William thumped against the top of the coach. "We've arrived at Urquhart Castle."

Fiona gazed over at C.C. and Michael. "Get ready to run. The door that leads you back to your time in history won't stay open for long."

C.C. swiped at her tear stained face and nodded.

Michael reached over and squeezed her hand. "Ready?"

She hesitated.

"I'm not ready either," he said.

William drove the coach toward a side entrance of the castle overlooking Loch Ness. The shadows of the night hid the castle's true condition. Before repeated attacks had reduced it to rubble, it had once been a mighty fortress, a guardian of the Highlands. Now only a few towers and walls remained to hint at its past glory.

The coach stopped beside a gravel path to a familiar tower and a wooden door painted with a Scottish thistle, the same door they'd come through earlier that evening. Golden light outlined the door, and mist curled around the threshold as the whole area glowed and pulsated in the moonlight.

Silently, the passengers filed out of the coach, each locked in their own inner turmoil.

"We're cutting this close," William said, breaking the silence. He looked past them in the direction of the forest, then toward the castle. "We're being watched."

"Only ghosts watch us, old friend," Liam said, clasping the older man on the shoulder. "The dead never rest near a battle, and Urquhart has seen more than its share. You drove like a banshee. No one followed us here." Liam pressed his hand against the wound as he tested his ability to move, rotating his shoulder. "Feels like the bullet went clean through."

Fiona examined his injury. "Stop doing that. You'll open the wound. When we get back, we'll have a doctor look at it."

"I don't need a doctor. I've survived worse." He kept his expression closed as he reached to take the rifle from C.C.

Bells from a nearby monastery began to toll the midnight hour. The sound vibrated through the frosted air. The door in the tower opened, seemingly by its own accord, as the faint sounds of a clock began its countdown.

One strike.

The church bells and the clock's deep-throated countdown joined together in warning.

A mist wound around C.C.'s ankles, chilling her to the bone.

Fiona cast her a gentle smile. "Don't worry. Everything will be all right." Fiona motioned toward C.C. and Michael. "We have to reach the twenty-first century before the clock is done striking. The two of you will go through first. Liam and I will follow close behind."

The clock's second strike chimed.

As C.C. approached the tower door, the mist rolled over the ground and seemed to push her forward. The glow over the entrance pulsated and grew brighter. She stepped over the threshold. The deep notes of the clock counting down the hour to midnight grew louder. It struck its third tone, and the mist rose higher, shutting out the light.

The temperature dropped. Teeth chattering, C.C. took another step and was engulfed in blinding white: white walls, white ceiling, and white floors. Disoriented, she couldn't tell which direction she should walk. Panic seized her. Was the floor moving?

Someone nudged her from behind. "Follow the sound of the grandfather clock."

The clock struck a sixth time. The sound pulled her forward.

C.C. stumbled into a room lined with mahogany paneling, red carpets, and wall-to-wall doors of every size and shape. Her mind registered that she'd returned, but she felt numb, and so cold she questioned if she'd ever feel warm again. She was back in the sisters' mansion.

Dizzy, she took another step and pitched forward.

Lady Roselyn caught her. "You're safe now."

"Safe?" C.C. regained her balance. The question went unanswered.

Michael was the next to appear, and he received a hug as well. William followed, with Fiona close behind him. Lady Roselyn's questions went unanswered as everyone else focused on the door as they waited for Liam's return.

The grandfather clock continued its countdown.

Seven.

Eight.

Nine.

Seconds ticked by. Fiona shouted Liam's name, her voice edged with panic.

Ten.

Fiona took a step toward the threshold. William and Lady Roselyn held her back. "He will make it," Lady Roselyn said.

Eleven.

But C.C. noted the uncertainty in William's and Lady Roselyn's expressions. William had said that he believed they were being watched. Liam had dismissed the idea, joking about ghosts. What if William had been right? What if Liam had been attacked?

Twelve.

The door slammed shut, plunging the room into

silence.

Fiona turned toward Lady Roselyn, a stricken expression in her eyes. "Open the door again. Liam hasn't returned."

Lady Roselyn shook her head slowly. "You know I can't. This door only makes itself available on New Year's Eve, and that time has passed. Liam is lost to us. Trying to bring him back now is too dangerous."

Chapter Twenty-Eight

C.C. caught Fiona before she collapsed on the floor. She wished she could comfort her and say Liam would be all right, but the truth was that C.C. didn't know for sure. Traveling back in time wasn't supposed to be possible, yet the three sisters had somehow unlocked the secret. The expression on both Fiona's and Lady Roselyn's faces said more than words ever could. Liam wasn't coming back.

"There has to be something we can do," C.C. said.

"My sister is right. It's too dangerous." Fiona straightened, her face broken with grief. She was a different person from the laughing barista C.C. had first met at the Matchmaker Café. Fiona shot Lady Roselyn a glance and said evenly, "We have rules."

Lady Roselyn reached for Fiona. "Liam knew the risks."

Fiona ignored her sister's outstretched hand as Bridget rushed into the room. Bridget was flushed, her hair piled on top of her head in wild disarray. Even her long gown was askew. One shoulder strap was broken and the other missing. "The reporters are right behind me," Bridget said under her breath. "I couldn't stop— What happened?"

Lady Roselyn frowned, taking in Bridget's appearance. "First, tell me what happened to you."

"One of the reporters was a little too grabby." Her

mouth edged up in a smile. "I pushed him into the River Ness."

"Good for you," Lady Roselyn said. Her gaze drifted over to Fiona, and she sighed. "We have very bad news. Our dear Liam didn't make it back in time."

Bridget gasped and covered her mouth to stifle her scream. Suddenly a wave of reporters flooded into the room. She stepped quickly aside to avoid being trampled.

Camera flashes lit up the already bright area. The next wave brought Tatiana, her mother, and Harold. They moved over to stand by a bank of windows. Their whole focus was trained on Michael.

Another round of flashes intruded. C.C. held up her arm to shield herself from their glare.

A reporter shoved a microphone toward Michael. It was the same man who had crashed their wedding. "Back so soon? We were told you were headed on your honeymoon to someplace warm."

"We missed the snow," Michael said.

C.C. knew the speech Michael had rehearsed. It would hint there was trouble in paradise, but that they were trying to work through their issues. The usual cliché. A woman reporter shoved a mic toward C.C. with a battery of questions, repeating the same ones a reporter had asked Michael. C.C. had no chance to say anything, even if she'd wanted to, before the woman reporter moved on to what was really on her mind: "Is Michael good in bed?"

Michael stepped between C.C. and the reporter. "Leave my wife alone. Ask me all the questions you want. Questioning my wife is off limits." He signaled for Harold, who whisked C.C. out of the room.

C.C. was thankful. She wanted it to be over. She wanted to go home.

Chapter Twenty-Nine

The next morning, Michael stood looking out the third-story window of the MacBride mansion, fingering the wedding ring C.C. had returned. He wished she hadn't. Somehow it felt right that C.C. should have his grandmother's ring.

A black taxicab pulled into view and parked in front of the entrance. A soft dusting of snow had begun to fall. The morning was gray and would only darken as the day aged.

C.C. was leaving today.

She emerged from the mansion and headed toward the taxi.

He and C.C. hadn't spoken since they'd returned from Scotland's distant past. There was really nothing they could say. Words wouldn't change the facts. Tatiana was pregnant with his child, and he wouldn't abandon her. He wouldn't do what his father had done. Michael would acknowledge the child as his. If Tatiana wanted them to get married, that's what they'd do. If she didn't, or if she wanted to wait, that was okay with him as well. The most important thing right now was what Tatiana wanted and what was best for their child.

Below, C.C. paused beside the open taxi door and glanced over her shoulder, lifting her gaze in the direction of where Michael stood at the window.

He wouldn't beg for her to stay. That wouldn't be

fair to either one of them. He'd made good on his promise, and Harold had taken care of the financial details. C.C. and her family wouldn't have to worry anymore about their father's care. As promised, there was also enough for C.C. to open her sandwich shop.

Everything had worked out the way it was supposed to. Not exactly a fairytale ending. In fairytales Cinderella married her prince and lived happily ever after. This was not that kind of story. Maybe not everyone deserved a happy ending.

C.C. gave him a wave and a thin smile.

He pressed his hand against the cold windowpane and watched her climb into the taxi and drive away. For once in his life he wished he really were made out of stone.

Chapter Thirty

A month later, Michael entered the Matchmaker Café in Inverness, shutting the door against the biting snowstorm outside. There weren't many customers today. No doubt people didn't want to brave the cold weather. New Year's Day had brought a series of snowstorms that seemed to have little intention of leaving anytime soon.

As he gazed around the café, he knew intellectually that this was the twenty-first century. There were times, however, when he almost expected to see Bonnie Prince Charlie sitting at one of the tables.

He blew on his hands, delaying his meeting with Harold and the barrage of questions that would begin with, "How are you doing?" and end with, "If you love C.C., fight to win her back." Michael considered Harold's questions inappropriate. His best friend knew Tatiana was pregnant. What was the man thinking?

In the end, he and C.C. had agreed to an annulment. It was the easiest and, considering the circumstances, the fastest.

Michael heaved a sigh, brushed the snow from his coat, and headed toward the counter to order his coffee.

"Hello, William," Michael said.

William smiled. "Good to see you, lad. What will it be? The usual?"

Michael nodded.

"I haven't seen much of Tatiana," William said, pouring Michael's coffee.

Michael reached into his wallet. "She and her mother went to a spa in Paris. I think that's where they said it was."

William handed Michael his cup. "The ladies do love their spas. Your friend Harold is already here." William motioned to a table in the corner. "He wanted me to tell you it was too cold to play football today."

Michael took a sip of coffee. Harold complained about the weather, but he never missed a chance to play. The ritual kept them grounded. Michael and he agreed it was a link to their past. He took another sip, sensing a change in the air. "Where's Fiona?"

"Good question. I haven't seen her in over a week. Every time I ask, Bridget and Lady Roselyn change the subject and ask me for more boxes. They leave for America soon, to open a café in the Northwest. I volunteered to help out until their cousins arrive. They'll run the café until the sisters return." He refilled Michael's cup. "Congratulations. I heard you got the part. What is the name of the movie?"

"*Highland Rebel*. I start tomorrow. The studio wants to take advantage of the snow while it lasts." Michael paid for his drink and took another sip. "Hopefully, the sisters' cousins have the same gift of creating the perfect combination of a good cup of coffee and a welcoming atmosphere."

William smiled, wiping down the counter. "Time will tell," he said with a wink. "Time will tell."

"Well, it was great meeting you, William."

"The pleasure was all mine, lad."

Michael smiled his thanks and headed to where

Harold was bent over a stack of papers. Michael slid down opposite his friend. "Do you ever take time off?" he asked with a smile.

Harold looked up. "Why are you smiling? You're freaking me out."

"I'm trying something new. You didn't answer my question. You need to take some time off. Maybe you should try one of the sisters' adventures. It could change your life."

"Travel back in time? Not on your life."

The door to the café burst open. Snow blew in on a swirling mass of wind. The few people in the café looked over at the commotion. Tatiana and her mother swept into the café, looking as different as night and day. Tatiana wore loose-fitting winter-white slacks and sweater under a pink wool cape, while Alba was dressed in black, with thigh-high boots, leggings, a cropped sweater, and a fur coat.

"I forbid it," Alba shouted. Alba's voice was shrill and as cold as the wind that had blown in. "Did you hear me?" Alba said, pulling off her leather gloves.

Tatiana spun around to confront her mother. "I heard you loud and clear. In fact, I've heard every word you've spoken to me from the first moment you realized that I was your meal ticket."

Customers in the café shrank back and concentrated on their beverages, trying not to look as though they were listening to the noisy confrontation.

Michael leaned over to Harold. "Do you know what's going on?"

Harold wore the classic Cheshire-cat grin. "A hunch. A very strong hunch."

Alba sucked in her breath. "How dare you refer to

yourself as my meal ticket! After all I've done for you! All I've sacrificed..."

Tatiana's voice was calm. "I'm grateful. You know I am. You've been repaid a thousandfold. You know that as well. It's time for you to let go and realize that I can manage my life on my own. I'm not saying I don't want you in my life. I just want you not to hold on so tight."

"You need me," Alba pleaded. "I know what's best for you. I always have."

Tatiana backed away from her mother. "I love him, and I won't give him up."

"We're back to him? So that's what this is all about." Alba pointed her finger at her. "He was a steppingstone. That's all he was, no more. He served his purpose."

Michael leaned over toward Harold. "Do you know who they're talking about? Are they talking about me? Am I being replaced?"

"Would you care?" Harold had a twinkle in his eye. "That's what I thought. No, they're talking about that husband she's never divorced, Darrell Grant."

"She still loves him?"

Harold's smile lit up his face. "Why do you think the both of them kept delaying signing the papers?"

"How long have you known?"

"More of a suspicion. While you and C.C. traveled back in time, I went to talk to Tatiana. There was something odd about her performance at the wedding that didn't ring true. When I found her, she was sobbing and clutching the divorce papers. Darrell had messengered them over to her. She said he'd given in to all of her demands. She also said that he'd written a note that said he wanted her to be happy."

"But she's having my child."

"Are you sure?" He motioned toward Tatiana.

"Listen to reason," Alba said. "You're having a baby."

Tatiana glanced at Michael. She paused for several heartbeats before she smiled, mouthed a thank you, and turned back to her mother. "I'm no longer going to lie to Michael."

"Think of your baby."

"I am. My child deserves to know who his father really is. I love Darrell, and he loves me."

"But the divorce papers…"

"I ripped them up and called him. We talked for hours. He arrives tonight. Do you hear me, Mother? I'm not going to give him up."

"But he's penniless. You could do so much better. Michael is…"

"I don't care how wealthy Michael is. I love Darrell. Now that Darrell's football career is over, he plans to go back to school. He wants to be a teacher and coach high school football."

"High school?" Alba said with scorn. She folded her arms across her chest. "You, a teacher's wife? I doubt on a teacher's salary Darrell could afford your brand of lipstick."

Tatiana leaned toward her mother. "Again, you're not listening. I. Don't. Care. Thanks to Harold, I've made good investments with the money I earned as a model. Plus, my shoe company is doing well. Even if all that went away, it wouldn't change how I feel about him."

Harold started chuckling.

"What's so funny?" Michael said.

"I also manage Darrell's finances. I swear the man must have some Scottish blood in him. He's as tight as you are sometimes. He doesn't care about fancy cars or owning homes on every continent, like some of the professional players. Darrell invested the lion's share of what he earned playing football. Darrell Grant is worth a fortune."

Chapter Thirty-One

Six months later, on a warm sunny summer's day and far from the Highlands of Scotland, C.C was putting the finishing touches on her shop, Sandwich Land. The shop was located in a thriving sales location just outside Seattle, and the grand opening was only a half hour away. Homemade bread cooled on racks, and the refrigerated cases were filled with a variety of cheeses, meats, and vegetables. C.C.'s dream had become a reality. Except that the saying from Michael's nana kept popping into her thoughts, like clouds that threatened to dampen a sunny summer day...

Dreams become real when they are shared with someone you love.

C.C. climbed up another rung on the ladder to hang the green-and-blue plaid curtains that were the same pattern as Michael's family tartan. She may have gone a little overboard with the Scottish theme, but if it weren't for Michael and her adventure in Scotland, her dream might never have become a reality. True to his word, Michael had given her a generous bonus, and along with the money she'd already saved, it had made it possible for her to open her shop.

But saying Michael's name, even in her thoughts, brought a lump to her throat. People got over relationships all the time. What was her problem? Why was it taking her so long? On the positive side of the ledger, she had purposely dived into not only making her dream a reality but had invited her sisters to be partners too. She'd also begun repairing her relationship with her dad. It hadn't been easy, and it was still ongoing, but they were making progress.

She and her sisters had found this retail location by accident. It had been created in the 1960s by a visionary who had a unique idea of how to preserve homes that had been built in the 1920s. He'd purchased and restored a variety of cottage-style homes, a few barns, and even a chicken coop, from all over the Seattle area, and moved them to this location, creating a popular retail village.

The home C.C. and her sisters had chosen came with the added bonus of a second story, which they turned into an apartment for their father. When they proposed the idea to him of living in the apartment, he jumped on the idea. He liked the plan so much that he offered to help get the shop ready as well as helping with the customers after the shop opened. He seemed in better spirits than at any time since their mother had passed away.

"Do you need some help?" Her sister Belle stood at the bottom of the ladder, gazing up toward her. Belle was the oldest of the three sisters and looked exactly like their mother, with short curly dark hair and bright green eyes.

"Almost done," C.C. called down.

Belle moved away from the ladder and peered out the front window, giving the street a good onceover. "There's a stretch limo parked outside. Are we expecting visitors?"

C.C. finished adjusting the curtains, pleased with

the results. "There are over thirty shops in the village. It's probably a tour group, or friends on a shopping spree."

"Could be," her sister said, absently, "except there's a hunky guy getting out of the limo."

"In the first place, men also shop, and in the second, you're engaged."

Belle stuck out her tongue at C.C. "I can still look." She turned back to the window, gasped, and then covered her mouth with her hands. Her hands dropped as she stepped from the window. "Oh. My. Gosh! Mr. Gorgeous is headed straight toward our shop."

C.C. tried to look out the window, but the curtain's valance blocked her line of vision.

"We can let him know that we don't open for another half an hour. I'm still waiting for Emma to bring over cookies from her bakery in the village. I want everything to be perfect. If the man can't wait, you can give him a brochure and let him know we deliver."

"Ah, huh." Her sister pulled her hair off her face and tucked in her shirt. "He looks familiar. Movie star familiar. Like the guy in that Scottish movie trailer we saw recently, starring your ex-boss. What was the name of the movie?"

C.C. gripped the top rung of the ladder. "*Highland Rebel.*" When she'd seen the beginning of the movie preview with her sister, C.C. had made an excuse to leave, saying she needed more chocolate from the concession counter. She knew if she stayed to watch the whole trailer, she'd burst into tears.

She'd signed the annulment papers and left Scotland without saying good-bye. She didn't trust herself to tell him what she really thought about him and Tatiana. They weren't right for each other. But she couldn't think of a way to say it that didn't sound self-serving.

Belle's eyes widened as she turned toward C.C. "You said he had a girlfriend."

"He does. She's probably waiting in the limo. They're expecting a baby."

"You also said you didn't have any feelings for him."

"I don't."

"Liar."

The brass bell over the door chimed, and in walked Michael Campbell. He filled the entrance.

That wasn't fair. He looked better than she remembered. C.C. backed down the ladder as all the feelings and memories she'd kept bottled up inside for the past six months rushed to the surface. The first time they'd met and he walked her home. Their first kiss. How worried he'd looked when he pulled her from the River Ness. How it felt to have his strong arms wrapped around her...

C.C. continued backing down the ladder. Her foot missed the rung and stepped out into air instead. She tumbled backwards, reaching out as she plummeted toward the floor with a scream.

And she landed in Michael's arms.

Chapter Thirty-Two

"Are you hurt?"

The rich timber of Michael's voice wrapped around her like a protective blanket. C.C. opened her mouth to speak, but nothing came out. She moistened her lips and pressed her hand against her chest, trying to slow the hammering of her heart. She'd missed the sound of his voice.

Michael had carried her over to a chair and set her down, along with the oversized open gym bag he'd been carrying. He gazed at her as though she were the only one in the room. "Your eyes are the color of warm honey."

"Belle," C.C. said in a voice that sounded suspiciously like a frog's croak. "Can you give Michael and me some privacy?"

Belle plopped down in a chair nearby. "Not a chance."

C.C. sent what she hoped was a threatening glare in her sister's direction. She knew it had missed the mark when her sister giggled and settled back against the chair as though she were preparing to watch a movie. The only thing missing was the popcorn. C.C. sighed and concentrated on Michael. "Why are you here?" She winced at how harsh her words sounded. She couldn't help it. She was trying to get over him, and she knew the moment she saw him that she'd failed miserably.

"I want to give you something," he said. "Several things, actually."

Searching for a distraction, C.C. glanced out the window. The press hadn't mentioned that he and Tatiana had married or that they'd had the baby. They might have been able to keep both a secret. Probably the wedding announcement would take place the night of the premier for *Highland Rebel*. "Is Tatiana in the limo? Isn't she due any day now?"

"She and Darrell had a healthy baby girl."

"Darrell? I thought they were getting a divorce."

"No," Belle answered. "I read that they were back together. Darrell and Michael also formed a foundation to mentor children without fathers. Seriously, you need to keep up with the news."

"And you should have told me," C.C. said to her sister through clenched teeth.

Belle batted her eyes in her signature innocent look. "You expressly told me not to mention Tatiana or Michael's names, under any circumstances. Even if they were swallowed up by a massive earthquake, abducted by aliens, or..."

C.C. groaned. "Got it. We'll discuss this later."

The gym bag wiggled, meowed, and then toppled over. A kitten peeked out, gazed toward C.C., and meowed again.

C.C. scooped the kitten into her arms. She was the image of the kitten she'd tried to rescue from the River Ness. Attached to the kitten was a collar with a charm that read *Nessie*. "She's adorable. Nessie looks so much like..."

"Like the one in Scotland," Michael finished. He took a deep breath. "As you heard, Tatiana and I are no longer together. We ended it. It turns out we were each in love with someone else. Tatiana with the man she was trying to divorce and me with a woman who lost a glass slipper. But I didn't come here just to bring you Nessie."

He pulled two cardboard boxes from the gym bag. One was sealed in plastic and the other box looked brand new. He handed her the one in plastic first. It had a news clipping attached that read, *"Crazy American football player dredges the River Ness looking for shoes."*

C.C. scratched the kitten under her chin. "Are they talking about you?"

"Guilty."

"These must be the wedding slippers I lost before you rescued me. I can't believe you found them." She began to unwrap the plastic, but he stopped her.

"You may not want to open the box. They're pretty smelly and gross. They've been in the water for hundreds of years. My first plan was to travel back in time to where you lost the shoes. Lady Roselyn said that was impossible. The door we traveled through wasn't available until next New Year's Eve. The only other door that opened to that exact time period was the door to the Culloden battlefield. Lady Roselyn said the key to that door was missing, and so was Fiona."

C.C. remembered how concerned Fiona had been when Liam had been shot and then when he hadn't returned. "I'm not surprised she went after him. Love is a powerful motivator. I hope she finds him. Were Lady Roselyn and Bridget worried?"

"They said they weren't, but I got a completely different vibe. Lady Roselyn said that Scotland has a strange effect on people. It brings out a person's true feelings, and sometimes the only course is to follow your heart. When I realized I couldn't travel back in time, and then discovered that your shoes were ruined, I had this brainstorm." He reached for the second box. "The originals were a mess, so I asked Tatiana if she would make you a duplicate pair."

Little Nessie jumped down from C.C.'s lap and sniffed the box. She meowed her approval as Michael lifted the lid. Inside was an exact replica of C.C.'s wedding shoes, the ones that reminded her of the glass slippers described in all the Cinderella stories she'd read or seen in the movies.

He grinned. "I'm searching for the woman of my dreams who can fit into these glass slippers."

"You went to a lot of trouble," she said under her breath.

"You are worth it."

She lifted her gaze, and then her mind numbed as she was lost in his smile. He was smiling. Full-on smiling. It took her a moment for that to register and then to realize that he was waiting for her to respond. "But why?"

"That's an interesting story," he said, kneeling down as he slipped off one of her shoes. "It seems that the woman I married ran away before I could tell her I loved her. I have a feeling she wouldn't have believed me even if I had tried, however. I decided I needed to make a grand gesture, like Prince Charming."

"The prince didn't make a grand gesture," C.C. said in a whisper.

"Of course he did. He'd fallen in love with a woman who'd lost a glass slipper and then vanished at

164

the stroke of midnight. He did what any man in love would do. He announced to the world that he would search the kingdom for the woman who fit the glass slipper and then ask her to marry him."

"That was risky," C.C. said. "In the entire kingdom, I'm sure there were at least one or two other women who wore the same shoe size. Plus, Cinderella wasn't a princess."

"Ah, but you're forgetting that they were enchanted glass slippers and would recognize their owner. Something the prince knew, being a prince and all. But I've also had a lot of time to think why the prince wanted to have all the women in the kingdom try on the shoe. I think that he already knew Cinderella wasn't a princess when he made his announcement. Otherwise, why go to all the trouble of going door to door? No, our prince was a smart man. He knew what he was doing. He was letting Cinderella know how important she was to him and the lengths he would go to, to prove his love. It didn't matter to him if she was from his world or not. He loved her." Michael lifted a slipper from the layers of tissue. "His proclamation to search the land was his grand gesture of love. Do you want to hear the story of a modern-day prince and his grand gesture?"

Belle picked up the kitten, which had wandered over to her, before she cleared her throat and raised her hand. "I do."

Michael's smile grew wider. "The prince in my story braved not only the icy cold waters of the River Ness but the dangerous monster that lurked in its depths."

C.C. raised her eyebrow. "Lurked?"

Michael gave a curt nod. "Lurked. I wonder if the Brothers Grimm had this much trouble with critics?"

She pressed her lips together, trying not to smile. "Sorry. Continue."

The brass bell over the door chimed again, and C.C.'s sister Briar Rose entered. "What's going on?"

Belle squealed with joy and motioned for Rose to join her. "It's Michael Campbell. I think he's going to ask our sister to marry him."

Rose rushed past C.C. to join Belle. "Michael Campbell? The quarterback?" Rose gazed over at Michael and then sat down in the chair beside Belle. "Isn't he Dad's favorite player? Should we ask Dad if he wants to watch too?"

"Maybe we should ask the whole village." C.C. offered.

Belle exchanged a glance with Rose. "Should we?"

C.C. buried her head in her hands. "This is not happening."

Michael pulled C.C.'s hands away from her face. "I don't care if your sisters invite your dad—or the whole world, for that matter. I'm in love with you. I've loved you from the moment we first met."

"Ask her," both Belle and Rose said at the same time. Little Nessie chimed in with a loud meow.

Michael took both of C.C.'s hands in his. "I love you, Cinderella Charming. Will you marry me?"

His words surged through her, releasing the emotions she'd kept under lock and key. She leapt into his arms, warmed by the love she saw reflected in his eyes. She held his gaze as the world drifted away.

The delighted screams of her sisters faded into the background. Somewhere she heard her father's voice as he walked down the stairs to ask why everyone was screaming. Somewhere she thought she heard the bell over the door chime as people entered her shop.

She smiled, her lips a breath away from his. "Yes, my prince, I will marry you."

A word about the author...

Pam Binder is an award-winning Amazon and *New York Times* Bestselling author. *Publisher's Weekly* has said, "Binder gracefully weaves elements of humor, magic and romantic tensions into her novels."

Drawn to Celtic legends and anything Scottish or Irish, Pam blends historical events, characters, and myths into everything she writes.

Pam is the president of the Pacific Northwest Writers Association, a conference speaker, and teaches two year-long novel-writing courses, "After the First Draft" and "Write Your Story." Pam writes historical fiction, contemporary fiction, and fantasy.

Visit her at:

http://pambinder.com